Far from You

LISA SCHROEDER

Simon Pulse
New York London Toronto Sydney

SIMON PULSE

An imprint of Simon & Schuster Children's Publishing Division
1230 Avenue of the Americas, New York, NY 10020
First Simon Pulse paperback edition January 2010
Copyright © 2009 by Lisa Schroeder
All rights reserved, including the right of reproduction in whole or in part in any form.
SIMON PULSE and colophon are registered trademarks of Simon & Schuster, Inc.
Also available in a Simon Pulse hardcover edition.
For information about special discounts for bulk purchases, please contact Simon & Schuster Special Sales at 1-866-506-1949 or business@simonandschuster.com.
The Simon & Schuster Speakers Bureau can bring authors to your live event. For more information or to book an event contact the Simon & Schuster Speakers Bureau at 1-866-248-3049 or visit our website at www.simonspeakers.com.
Designed by Mike Rosamilia
The text of this book was set in Adobe Garamond.
Manufactured in the United States of America
2 4 6 8 10 9 7 5 3 1
The Library of Congress has cataloged the hardcover edition as follows:
Schroeder, Lisa.
Far from you / Lisa Schroeder. — 1st Simon Pulse ed.
p. cm.
Summary: A novel-in-verse about sixteen-year-old Ali's reluctant road trip with her stepmother and new baby sister, and the terror that ensues after they end up lost in the snow-covered woods.
ISBN 978-1-4169-7506-9 (hc)
1. Novels in verse. 2. Stepfamilies—Fiction. 3. Survival—Fiction.] I. Title.
PZ7.5.S37Far 2009
[Fic]—dc22
2008025268
ISBN 978-1-4169-7507-6 (pbk)
ISBN 978-1-4169-8988-2 (eBook)

day four

We're alone
with only
the cold
and dark
to keep us
company.

I know them
so well now,
they're like
old friends.

Familiar.

Old friends
who have stayed
too long
and need to go.

I wish
the angel
would have stayed.

For a second,
I felt warmth.
I felt safe.
I felt love
as she whispered
my name,
"Alice,"
and floated
toward me
before she
disappeared.

Was I dreaming?
Hoping?
Hallucinating?

So hungry.
So tired.

Cold.

I look out the window,
and although it's dark,
the moon
illuminates the scene
as if a faraway
floodlight
is hung
from the sky.

So much whiteness.
Everywhere.

Come back,
angel.

Let us fly
away
from
here.

Please.
Come back.

softly snowing

Memories
fall
like
snowflakes
upon
my dreams.

Me and Mom,
a piece of art,
a promise,
a hug.

Me and Dad,
a thousand tears,
a bouquet,
a loss.

Me and Blaze,
an autumn day,
a walk,
a kiss.

Me and Claire,
a flowing skirt,
a song,
a fight.

The snowflakes
toss and tumble,
each different
and yet
the same.

The snowflakes
of my life.

part 1

everything's always
changing

here she comes

Muffled voices
outside my door
that October morning
woke me
and took me
from a peaceful place
to one I'd come
to hate.

When one of them
stepped into my room,
the hallway light
landed on my
closed eyelids,
urging them
to open
like a hand
pulling on a
doorknob.

"It's time," Dad said.

I didn't open my eyes.
I didn't move.
I didn't speak.

"Ali, you awake?"

I gave a little grunt.

The event
wasn't worth
wasting breath on.

"We'll call you later.
When she's here."

Pause.

"I love you," he said
quickly and quietly.

It's pretty sad
when you have to
think about it
before you say it.

just breathe

The clock read
4:13 a.m.

My dog, Cobain,
slept at the foot
of my bed.

I changed directions
and curled up
next to his warm body,
feeling the rhythm
of his breathing.

I stroked his golden fur,
and my heartbeats
s o f t e n e d.

He breathed.
I breathed.

Soon my breaths
were slow and steady,
in sync with his.

Cobain.
My oxygen tank.

He breathed.
I breathed.

The garage door
rumbled open
beneath me.

They were gone.

Gone until
they'd come back
with her.

Then there'd be   me.

He breathed.
I breathed.

They knew her name.
But they wouldn't tell me.
It'll be a surprise, Victoria had said,
like a surprise is a *good* thing.

My stepmom.
Victoria.

She reminded me
of a chameleon lizard,
with her annoying habit
of curling her tongue up
just slightly,
and touching her top lip,
when she was
concentrating.

A chameleon.
One minute sweet as chocolate cake.
The next, sour and possessive,
like an old banker.

Once upon a time
he and I were close.
Dad.

We'd cook together,
watch basketball together,
and make up silly jingles together,
since advertising
is his line of work.

Things changed.
Victoria moved in.
He changed.

It's like he tried

to move on
to greener pastures,
but the tractor in the barn,
once adored,
became a nuisance
and kept him connected
to the painful past.

I squeezed in closer
to Cobain.

He breathed.
I breathed.

I could see Dad
holding his new
baby girl.

Smiling.
Happy.
Totally in love.

He'd breathe.
She'd breathe.

Then there'd be   me.

the short version

Mom got cancer.
Cancer sucks.
She died.
Dad remarried.
The end.

our time is now

After a while
I got up,
showered,
and put on my favorite jeans,
a white shirt,
my black jacket,
and my combat boots.

I grabbed my battered,
scuffed-up
guitar case
and headed outside.

The sunlight streamed
through the tree in our front yard,
lighting up the yellow leaves,
creating a brilliant
golden statue
that moved magically
when the breeze blew.

Amazing.

I love fall.
Fall in Seattle.
The season of
warm colors.

I thought about calling Blaze,
to see if I could talk him into going,
but he likes church
about as much
as the queen likes profanity.

It's the one thing
between us
that feels like
a tiny splinter
in your foot.

Painful and annoying,
but difficult to remove.

Blaze and I met
at a concert
last spring.

Our eyes locked
just as Mudhoney
took the stage,
and it was like a rocket
blasting off
into space.

I felt heat
and my body trembled
and forces
beyond my control
pulled me
to him
as the music ripped
through our bodies.

I didn't know his name.
He didn't know mine.
And yet,
it was like
we'd known each other
forever.

My best friend, Claire,
was with me,
and she kept trying
to pull me away,
like she was afraid
for my life.

Silly girl.
Nothing to worry about.

If anything,
he sparked
a fire
inside of me,
making me want
to live
again.

the peace I need

I pulled up in my old Nova.
Claire got in
wearing a long, flowing purple skirt
and a silky, smooth black blouse.

She makes
all of her own
clothes.

Fashion
is her
passion.

I think she
should be a singer.

She's the voice
to the music we make
at church.

Like hot cocoa
and a soft blanket
and fuzzy slippers,
warming you up
top to bottom.

Raspy and sweet
all at the
same time.

I used to envy her,
but then I decided
to just be thankful
for making
incredible music
together.

My music
was complete
because of Claire.

She got in
and threw a CD
in my lap.

"Your turn to listen."

The church we go to,
Center for Spiritual Living,
makes CDs
of the sermons
and the music.

After I backed out,
I looked at Claire,
but my smile
didn't want to come out
and play.

"What's wrong?" she asked.

She knows me
like a druggie knows
his best vein.

"They went to the hospital.
Early this morning."

She gave a nod
of understanding.
I drove
in silence.

That is,
until she reached over
and popped the CD in the player
Blaze had installed for my birthday.

We listened to her sing
the words:

Pain in your heart.
You're playing the part
of a human in need.
You beg and you plead
Wash it away.
Wash it away.
Give me the peace,
the peace I need.

I wrote that song.

Funny how
time goes on,
things change,
and yet,
some things stay
exactly the same.

me and God

It's not that I'm
super-religious or anything.

In fact,
the Center for Spiritual Living
is not about religion.

Otherwise
it'd be called
the Center for Religious Living.

There's a difference.

I like it because
there isn't any
bullshit there.

They let me be
who I am,
and understand
that it's all about
staying
connected
to the source.

I've been going
for as long
as I can remember.

It was my mom's church.
She played the guitar and sang.

Dad hardly ever went with her.
But she'd take me,
and I'd sit in the audience,
hypnotized
by her voice.

Magical.

She's the reason
I'm in love
with music.

It's one
of the many gifts
she gave me.

She probably
helped give me
my love for
God too,
even though I get
mad at him sometimes.

Kinda like my dad.

I get mad at him a lot.
Still, I can't help
but love him too.

holes of the heart

After church
we went out
for doughnuts
and coffee.

Claire loves
chocolate coconut ones.
She likes to dip them
in her coffee,
and then coconut flakes
float on the top
like icicles
bobbing down
a muddy river.

I like the holes.
The little rejects
that aren't
as alluring
but are just as
sweet.

"I'm sewing my dad's bowling shirt this afternoon,"
Claire told me.

"A bowling shirt?"

She shrugged. "He joined a league.
His team wants cool shirts.
I said I'd make him one.
If they like it, I'll make them for the whole team."

"Claire.
A bowling shirt?
What's next?
A fishing vest?"

She reached over
and took one of my
powdered-sugar
doughnut holes.

"Shut up.
It's cool. I swear.
I'll show you."

Claire didn't put
the entire hole
into her mouth.

She took a bite,
and her lips
were suddenly white,
like she kissed
a snowman
and he kissed her back.

I pictured this girl
with white lips
sewing bowling shirts,
and it made me laugh.

She grabbed another hole
and dabbed it on my cheeks.

I squealed and started
to do the same,
when my phone rang.

We froze,
doughnut holes
midair.

It rang.
And rang.

"Maybe it's Blaze," she said.

I glanced at the number.
I shook my head.
I stuffed the doughnut hole in my mouth.

The phone kept ringing.
Claire gave me a look.

"I'm eating!" I mumbled.

Finally
the ringing
stopped
and I noticed
my heart felt heavy,
like the holes
were stuck
right
there.

Holes in my heart.

Yeah.

That was about right.

what to do?

As I drove Claire home,
she talked,
trying to get my brain
to think about other things.

It didn't work.

"Want to come in?"
she asked when I pulled in the driveway.

I shook my head.

"Come on.
Don't you want to see the bowling shirt?"

I smiled.

"Sorry, Claire," I said.
"Forgive me?"

She reached over for a hug.
I liked her answer.

"Go see Blaze," she said.
"Don't go home and just sit there."

She's smart,
that girl.

"And check your messages," she said as she got out.

Okay.
Maybe
too smart.

the good stuff

Blaze's mom, Ginger, let me in
and pointed to the garage,
which meant
that's where he was.

She doesn't like me.

Blaze keeps telling me I'm imagining it.
I say I'm right.

When I learned she's a tattoo artist,
I wanted her to give me one.
She's given Blaze seven.

I wanted a little heart
on my chest
like Janis Joplin
supposedly had.

Dad would never know.
Still, she wouldn't do it.
She used my age as an excuse.
Whatever.

She doesn't talk to me.
Never says, "Hi, Ali, how are you?"
Or "Ali, want to stay for dinner tonight?"
Or "Ali, I hear you're going to be a sister."

Nothing.

Like that day.
No talking.
Just pointing.

Blaze was banging
on his drum set,
the music from the stereo
blasting so loud,
I wondered
if he could hear
himself play.

I stood there,
him oblivious
to anything
but the music.

I love to watch him play.

Muscles urging.
Passion surging.
Anger purging.

So. Powerful.

When the song ended,
I walked over,
and from behind,
I slipped my arms
around his tattoo-covered chest,
leaned down,
and kissed his neck.

He took my hand
and with a hundred kisses,
walked his lips
up my arm.

"Surprise," I whispered in his ear.

He stood up,
turned around,
and then
the world disappeared
as I was swept up
and away
into the world
of Blaze.

Muscles urging.
Passion surging.
Anger purging.

So. Amazing.

almost the perfect day

I got my guitar.

We played.
We kissed.
We danced.
We kissed.
We talked.
We kissed.
We sang.
We kissed.

I almost forgot
everything else.

Almost.

the best

Finally
I told him.

"I think I'm a sister today."

"You think?"

"Dad called.
I didn't answer."

He looked at me
with his
chocolate brown eyes
and it's like
his love
radiated through me
so strongly,
I started
to sweat.

"Want me to listen for you?" he asked.

That is why I have
more love
than my heart
can possibly hold
for Blaze.

He is
better than warm fall colors,
better than beautiful music,
better than doughnuts and coffee.

At that moment,
I couldn't think of one single thing
better
than Blaze.

oh, so gently

We went to his room.
He listened to the message.

When he was done,
he kissed me softly,
with such tenderness,
it almost brought me
to tears.

Then he wrapped
his strong arms
around me
and whispered in my ear,
"Her name is Ivy.
And she has the best big sister ever."

before, after, and somewhere in-between

Blaze and his mom
were going out to dinner
with Blaze's older brother and his brother's wife.

I wanted to go too.
But Ginger didn't invite me.

It was hard to for me to leave,
because I knew
it'd be a while
before I'd see Blaze again.

We don't go to the same school,
and I'm so jealous of the girls
who kiss their boyfriends
before every class.
Lucky girls.

So, after we said good-bye,
I headed home,
thinking it would just be
me and Cobain
eating mac 'n' cheese.

But Dad was there.

He looked happier
than I'd ever
seen him.

"I thought you could come to the hospital," he said.
"We can all spend the evening together.
You can meet your baby sister.
She's adorable, Al."

Perfect.

The kid wasn't even a day old
and the one big, happy family thing
had already begun.

"I have homework, Dad.
I can't."

He tried to convince me
I could skip it,
or bring it with me,
or do it in the morning before school,
but I played the part of
concerned student,
and finally
he let up.

"You want something to eat?" he asked me,
and suddenly
it was like it was before.
Before *she* came along.

"Yeah.
I'm hungry."

I had visions of us
at the counter,
making dinner
together.

We'd boil the noodles
and mix up the sauce,
throwing in a little bit of this
and a whole lot of that.

And then we'd sit down
at the table
together.

Just me
and him.

I thought, Maybe he'll ask about school.
Maybe he'll ask about my music.
Maybe he'll ask about Blaze.

He reached for his wallet.
"Why don't you have a pizza delivered?
I have to get back to the hospital."

He handed me a twenty.
"We'll be home tomorrow."

And then he left,
taking any hunger
I might have had
right along with him.

the long version

When I came home
from school that day
so long ago,
Mom told me to sit down
and she'd get me some
milk and cookies.

She was a morning kindergarten teacher
and was always there
when I came home.

But she was also an artist,
and in the afternoons
she'd usually be in her studio,
painting.

At that time,
she'd been busy
painting pictures
for the owners of
a bed and breakfast
who wanted an
Alice in Wonderland room.

Mom loved the project because
Alice's Adventures in Wonderland
was her all-time
favorite book.

She even named me
after Alice.

The snickerdoodles,
fresh from the oven,
were warm
and comforting,
just like
a mother's love.

She sat and
watched me eat
while I babbled on
about this thing
and that thing.

When I saw
a single,
lonely tear
escape
before she could
reach up
and catch it,
I stopped talking,
suddenly aware
of how the cookies
were made
to soften the blow
of whatever
was coming next.

I don't remember
much of anything
after she said
the words
"pancreatic cancer,"
but I do know she kept saying,
like, every other sentence,
I'm going to fight this,
I'm going to fight this,
I'm going to fight this.

She had surgery,
and she went through chemo,
and she drank green juice every day,
and she
just
got
sicker.

I know she fought.
She fought hard.
But she didn't win.

The cancer won.

It didn't just win,
it basically
beat the shit
out of her.

Beat the shit
out of all of us.

Lost Without You

**a song
by Alice Andreeson**

*It's not supposed
to happen this way.
You're supposed to be here
each day and every day.
Like the leaves on the trees,
the stars and the moon;
they may disappear
but they come back soon.*

*Why'd you have to leave me?
Why'd you have to die?
I'm lost without you,
like the sun without the sky.
Lost without you,
I don't want to say good-bye.*

People around me,
they just don't understand.
They think time will help,
like it's a helping hand.
Time just hurts
'cause the memories all fade.
I want to see your face
and your lovely hair grayed.

Why'd you have to leave me?
Why'd you have to die?
I'm lost without you,
like the sun without the sky.
Lost without you,
I don't want to say good-bye.
I don't want to say good-bye.

Don't make me say

good-bye.

a gift of love

I played my music for a while,
and when I stopped,
I sat on my bed
and soaked in
the silence,
realizing that soon
the house would be filled
with the noise
of a baby.

I got up
and stepped
into the hallway.

I closed my eyes
and I could almost see Mom
coming from her bedroom,
on her way to give me
a good-night hug.

Every night,
for as long as I could remember,
she'd hug me
and whisper in my ear,
"Sweet dreams, my love."

It reminded me . . .

I turned
and went back
to my room.

Tucked in my closet
was a hidden secret,
underneath
the pants that were too short
and the sweaters that were too tight.

A painting
she gave me
two weeks
before she left us.

I didn't tell
anyone.

It's all mine.
Her final gift
to me.

I pulled it out,
and it was like
the day she gave it to me
all over again.

In the painting
the sky is dark,
with twinkling stars
and a glowing moon,
and down below
is a house
with a girl,
her chin resting in her hands,
looking out the window,
up at the sky.

And if you look closely,
the stars
form an outline
of an angel.

The words in the corner
of the painting say,
Find the gift in the little things.
And remember, Alice, I am with you always.

could it be?

They turned her studio
into the baby's room.

They didn't say anything
to me.

They just did it.

I would have taken
that room
on the first floor.

The room
that was so much
like Mom.

But they didn't
ask me.

I didn't speak to them
for days
after I found out.

I remember
walking in,
seeing the crib,
the changing table,
and the pink-and-blue
baby quilt
hung on the wall.

It all looked
so different.

Except for the ivy.

Mom had painted
delicate ivy
all around the walls,
just below the ceiling.

Then it hit me.

Is that where they got
the idea
for her name?

Seriously?

spicy

When I got home
from school on Monday,
no one seemed to notice
when I walked in the door.

I went to the kitchen
and got myself
a Diet Dr Pepper and
some chips and salsa,
hoping to
spice up my mood.

Newborn cries
came spiraling
down the
stairs.

I checked the label
on the jar.

Extra hot.

Good.

I needed all
the spicy
I could get.

doesn't add up

Eventually
they made their way
downstairs
and found me.

Victoria held
a little pink blob
in her arms.

"Do you want to hold her?" Dad asked me.

"I'm coming down with a cold.
I better not."

I got up,
put the dishes in the sink,
and started to go
to my room.

"She's your sister, Ali," Victoria said.

Was a statement like that
supposed to flip a switch
inside of me,
so suddenly
a bunch of sisterly love
would just come
shining through?

I turned around.
"She's not my sister.
She's my half sister.
There's a difference."

"Ali—"

But I didn't let him finish.
I left.

Because last time
I checked my math book,
half
does not equal
whole.

do I have to go to school?

The next morning,
I was a sloth,
tired
and
slow.

The baby cried
all
night
long.

I considered staying home
until I realized
at home,
there was a baby.

At school,
there was no baby.

So
I went.

do I look like I care?

Even at school
I couldn't get away
from the baby.

At lunch
Claire drilled me.

Is she cute?
Who does she look like?
Does she have hair?

I finally said,
"Claire, just stop, okay?
I don't know, because I don't give a crap."

"Sorry," she mumbled.

"Let's talk about something else."

So she told me
about the latest designs
she was working on,
and showed me
some sketches.

Who knew
I could be so interested
in fashion?

thank God for Johnny

When I got home
from school that day,
Victoria was on the sofa,
crying louder
than the damn baby.

Pathetic.

I searched the house for Dad,
but he was gone
or hiding
or something.

I thought,
If she thinks
I'm going to give her
the gift of sympathy,
she's off her
glider rocker.

"Ali?"
she sobbed.

I realized
I shouldn't
have come
home.

I should have driven
across town
to see Blaze.

Maybe I should just
move
across town.

"Ali,"
she cried,
"please!"

I went back
into the family room,
and she yelled
over the baby,
"Please. Take her.
Just for a few minutes?
I need a break.
I need to pee!"

"Put her in her crib.
Maybe she'll sleep."

"She won't.
She's hungry."

"Then give her a bottle."

Dumb ass.

She stood up.
"I'm nursing.
I can't give her a bottle.
I just have to wait until my milk comes in."

"Fine," I said.

Like a football player,
Victoria passed that baby off,
then dashed away.
I imagined her
doing a touchdown dance
in the hallway.

I walked around the family room,
the baby against my shoulder,
wailing.

"Welcome to the world, girlie.
It's not all sunshine and roses, is it?
Yeah, I know.
It sucks.
Get used to it."

I turned the stereo on
and cranked it.

It was "Slide"
by the Goo Goo Dolls.

I took Johnny Rzeznik's advice
and slid
across the hardwood floors
in big strides,
like I was skiing.

Singing
      and sliding.

         Singing
            and sliding.

                  Singing
                     and sliding.

Johnny is just
the best guy ever,
because
it wasn't long
before she was sleeping,
exactly
like a baby
should be.

now what?

I sat down
when the next song came on
because my legs
were done sliding
for the day.

I started to move her
off my shoulder,
because I had work to do,
but I didn't.

She was sleeping.

Even I know
you don't move
a sleeping baby.

At least it was a
better excuse
than the dog
ate my homework.

you're welcome

Victoria came back later
and turned the radio down.

She looked at me
with her tongue curled up,
her arms crossed,
and her eyes narrow and hard,
like she'd had her purse stolen
from a creepy guy
on the street.

"What'd you do?" she asked.

"I slid and sang."

"Give her to me."

"You sure?" I asked.

She reached down
and scooped her up
like a little kitten.

She was lucky.
The kitten kept on sleeping.

I got up
and headed to my room.

No "Thanks, Ali."
No "Great job, Ali."
No "I owe you one, Ali."

No nothing.

Even when
my dad wasn't around,
it was like she felt
threatened by me
or something.

I wanted to scream at her,
This isn't a competition!

But maybe
that's exactly
what it was.

woof

Victoria
didn't ask me
to take the baby
the rest of the week.

Mama Kitty
was pretty much
making me out to be
a
big,
bad
dog.

where's my fairy godmother?

The pile of homework
grew bigger
and bigger
over the next few weeks.

I was distracted.
I couldn't concentrate.

Ivy this
and Ivy that
and help make dinner
and do some laundry
and could you run to the store.

Unbelievable.

Finally,
on a Saturday,
I locked myself in my room
and attempted to conquer
two essays, a research paper,
and a gazillion pages of
geometry.

That is,
until Prince Charming
came to my rescue.

I changed out of my Cinderella rags
into my Lucky jeans.
No glass slippers, unfortunately.

When I got downstairs,
Blaze was holding Ivy
and talking and laughing
with Victoria.

"Did you know Vic was in a band?" he asked.

I shook my head.

"They were called The Lipstick Lunatics.
Isn't that an awesome name?"

I wanted to say,
Well, the lunatic part sounds about right.
But I refrained.

"I thought I told you," she said,
like we'd been best friends forever.

"What'd you play?" I asked.

"Keyboards.
Very badly, I might add."

"Hey, Ali," Blaze said,
"maybe you guys could play—"

I didn't let him finish.

"Give the baby back and come upstairs."

My tone told him
I was *not*
joking around.

"Leave your door open," she shouted after us.

Wicked
stepmother
indeed.

trust in me

I thought
when Dad
met Blaze,
he'd be worried.

That he'd see
the longish hair
and the tattoos
and think
he was one
bad
dude.

But all Dad said to him was,
"I trust you with Ali.
Break that trust, and you'll never see her again."

And that was that.

Dad told me later,
Mom had lots of talks with him
about raising a daughter.

He said
she told him
smothering me
would kill me.

My mom
knew me
so well.

is that on the SATs?

I don't know
when Blaze does
his homework.

He never talks about school.
At all.

When I talk about colleges
and which ones
to apply to,
since it's only a couple years away,
he never joins in.

One time I asked him
what he wants to do.

He said, "Plain and simple.
Rock star, baby."

So when I asked Prince Charming
if he could help me
with geometry,
it shouldn't have surprised me
when he said,
"Math really isn't my thing."

"What is your thing?"
I asked.

Then he pulled me to him,
nibbled on my ear,
and said,
"You."

yes or no?

Blaze works at
a used-record store.

Apparently
a guy came in earlier that day
who had a perfect copy
of an English release
of the Beatles'
Magical Mystery Tour album.

They gave him twenty bucks for it,
and the dude was thrilled.

It's worth
at least
a hundred.

Blaze loves it
when people are
stupid.

I told him
he should move in
to my house.

"By the way," he told me,
"I have Friday off."

"You do?" I squealed.
"Can we go out?"

"Can't think of anyone else
I'd rather spend my seventeenth birthday with," he said.

"Your birthday!
Shit, I totally forgot.
I have to get you a present."

"There's only one thing I want," he said
in a low, husky voice
before he kissed me.

"Blaze—"

"Don't say anything.
Just think about it, okay?
I love you.
You love me.
Just think about it."

I sighed. "Okay."

Just think about it.

Which meant
think about it,
and then say yes.

Right?

getting jerky with it

Monday at school.
I was telling Claire
about Blaze's visit.

"He was bonding with Victoria."

"Well, she seems all right, Ali.
Maybe you just need to get to know her better."

Seriously?

"Claire, you don't know what it's like.
What she's like.
She hates me, I think."

She started to reply,
then changed her mind.

She handed me
a piece of her jerky.

"Forgive my jerkiness?" she asked.

It made me giggle.
Claire is better
than Tickle Me Elmo
that way.

"So," I told her,
"Blaze wants to—you know.
For his birthday."

She nodded.
She didn't have to say anything.
I knew where she stood on the subject.

Abstinence.

Yeah,
she thinks
it's best to
wait,
wait,
and then
wait some more.

Although,
I have to wonder,
how do you know
where you really stand
until you have someone
you're madly in love with?

She hasn't really
had that yet.

"So, will he get what he wants?" she asked.

I shrugged.
"I'm still thinking on that."

She nodded again.
Took another bite of jerky.
Then she pointed the remaining stick at me.
"He's not being jerky about it, is he?"

I laughed again and shook my head.

I held up my candy bar.
"He's a sweetie, Claire.
You know that."

Then she got all serious.

"Ali, I know it must be hard.
If you want to talk to my mom—"

"No. It's okay.
I'll figure it out."

I like her mom,
but I couldn't imagine
talking to her mom
about THAT.

But she probably figured
the only thing worse
than talking to her mom
about it
would be talking to my dad
about it.

And she'd have been
exactly right
about THAT.

on the tip of my tongue

Wednesday night
Victoria went out
for a little while
with some friends,
leaving the three of us
alone.

I'd been wondering
about Mom
and her first time
and who it was with
and what it was like.

She met Dad
in college.

Was he the first?
If he wasn't,
would he know who was?
Would he even tell me?

As he fed Ivy,
I started to ask him.

As he bathed Ivy,
I started to ask him.

As he dressed Ivy,
I started to ask him.

When he noticed me
hanging around,
he asked, "You want to rock her?"

He thought I wanted to spend time
with her.

He didn't know I wanted to spend time
with him.

I didn't rock her.
And I didn't ask him.

getting personal

Homework
was conquered
and destroyed,
so as a reward,
Claire and I made plans
to get together.

Thursday after school,
I went to her house,
guitar in hand,
thinking we'd practice
our music.

The basement belongs to Claire.

One corner has
a table,
a sewing machine,
and a mannequin.

The other corner has
a piano
and a sofa,
where we sit
and play music.

I strummed on my guitar,
showing her
what I'd been working on.

She shook her head.

"What?" I asked.
"What's wrong?"

She looked at me.
Her eyes were like blocks of ice.
Cold and hard.

"You just keep writing the same sad stuff, Ali."

I shrugged. "So?"

"Mom says the people at church are talking."

"Talking?"

"They want to celebrate God.
They want to love Him and thank Him.
They want something different.
And to be honest, so do I."

"What are you saying?"

"It's too sad.
You've been writing this sad crap for long enough.
It's time to move on."

I felt like my best friend
had just pushed me
down
the
s
   t
      a
         i
           r
             s

"Sad crap?
Is that what you think of my music?"

"Come on, you know I don't mean it like that.
But we need to take a break.
I've already told them at church.
It's done."

Then she stood up
and went to the piano.
Her fingers danced
across the keys,
light and airy,
like nothing
was even wrong.

I thought of Mom.
How could I stop playing?
It was the one place
that hadn't changed.
The one place where
I felt her with me
no matter what.

"They've found someone else to play," she continued.
"For a while."

"Claire, what the hell?"

She shrugged.
"I want to focus on my clothing designs anyway."

I was so pissed,
I almost threw
my precious guitar
across the room,
smashing
the mannequin
to pieces.

But I didn't.
I just squeezed it,
looking at the girl
I thought I knew.

When she said, "You need to let God in, Ali,"
it felt like she was rubbing
sandpaper
up
    and
        down
    my
skin.

"What does that mean?" I asked.

"Come on. You know.
Write about something else.
Write about the good stuff!"

As if sadness
can be thrown,
like a small stone,
into a raging river
and quickly
forgotten.

I can't help it
if Mom is there,
in my music.
She brought me to it
in the first place.

I squeezed my fists
tightly around the guitar neck.

I squeezed so hard,
the strings
cut into
my hands.

There was nothing
I could think of to say,
because she'd probably
never understand.

And so
I just
left.

not a solo artist

When I got home,
I called Blaze
and we talked.

Well, I talked, shouted, and screamed.
He listened.

When I finally
shut up for a minute,
he said,
"You can play your music for me anytime.
You don't need that church messing with your mind
anyway."

"Blaze, please don't."

"What? It's the truth.
I swear, that place is like a cult."

And here
was the damn splinter,
getting deeper,
hurting more and more.

I've learned
the best thing to do
is change the subject.

"I know I can still play my music," I told him.
"It's just not the same without Claire.
But how can we ever play again?
She called my music crap."

"I'm sorry, baby.
I'm sure she'll get over it,
and you'll be doing your thing together again soon."

Blaze is right
about a lot of things.

But I was pretty sure
he wouldn't be right
about that.

not hungry

Friday at school
was weird.

Weird like
mashed potatoes
without gravy
or
a hot dog
without mustard.

It wasn't
how it was supposed to be.

I couldn't figure out
if Claire and I
were fighting
or fine
or what?

I went to the library
at lunch
and worked on
a science project,
while hoping
I wouldn't be gravyless
for long.

foul

When Dad got home from work,
he yelled at me
because I had forgotten to pick up
his dry cleaning
on my way home
from school.

His green eyes,
with big, dark bags
underneath them,
scowled at me
as he told me
how much the family
needed me to be
a team player.

"Dad," I screamed, "I didn't forget on purpose!"

Then I ran up the stairs
to get ready for my date,
thinking what a
rotten coach
my father
made.

the answer

That night,
Blaze picked me up
looking like
he just stepped out
of *Rolling Stone* magazine.

Hot.

"Blaze," Dad said, coming up behind me at the door,
"want to come in for a few minutes?"

"He can't," I said.
"We have, uh, dinner reservations.
Bye."

I stepped out
onto the porch
and shut the door
behind us,
before they had a chance
to say anything else.

"You in a hurry?" he asked.
"And should I take that as a good sign?"

I smiled. "In a hurry to get out of there, is all."

He pulled me close,
gave me a squeeze and a kiss,
and whispered,
"I'm excited to be with you, too.
I love you so much, Ali."

And in that moment,
knowing completely and fully
that no one
understood me
or loved me
more than Blaze,
I heard my soul whisper
yes.

hold on tight

Italian food
is Blaze's favorite.

I remember that night so clearly;
I can smell the oregano and garlic
and hear the buzz of conversation
wafting through the restaurant.

We talked and laughed
over plates of
angel hair pasta piled high
with tangy marinara sauce
and fresh parmesan cheese
sprinkled on top.

Blaze twirled the noodles
around his fork, and I thought,
Those noodles are like me,
wrapped around
Blaze's little finger.

We shared a bowl
of spumoni ice cream,
one bite for him,
one bite for me,
and so on,
until the little silver bowl
sat empty
between us.

When I pulled his gift
from my coat pocket,
he smiled
like a five-year-old
on Christmas.

"Happy birthday."

Blaze dreams
of the day
he rides off
into the sunset
on a Harley,
so I was thrilled
to find
the vintage
Harley Davidson key chain
on eBay.

He turned it
over and over
in his hands,
admiring its beauty
and the words
I had engraved
on the back.

Another year ahead.
Ready, set, go.
Please take me with you.
Love, Ali.

Then
Blaze's hands
reached across the table
and cradled my face.

"Of course you can come with me," he said.

An image of me and him
on a Harley,
riding far, far away,
popped into my head.

And I wished
I had bought him
the motorcycle
to go along
with the key chain.

what does it mean?

With happy hearts
and stuffed bellies,
we left the restaurant
and walked out
into the drizzly night.

As we approached his car,
Blaze pulled me to him
and kissed my neck,
sending tingles
up

and

down   and   sideways

through
my
body.

"I got us a room," he told me.
"At the MarQueen Hotel.
We can stay for a few hours,
then I'll take you home."

I kissed his delicious lips again
and tried to imagine myself
tangled in sheets
with the boy I love
in the old and charming
MarQueen Hotel.

"That's sweet," I said.

"Your first time should be sweet," he said
as he unlocked my car door,
"like freshly baked cookies.
Or spumoni ice cream.
I want it to be special, Al."

And when he said that,
for some reason,
I thought of Mom
and those cookies she'd made me
on that miserable day.

Suddenly,
no matter how much love
was in my heart
for Blaze,
I felt
empty.

As empty
as the ice cream dish
we had just
left
behind.

mixed-up

I should have felt
good.
Happy.
Excited.

I wanted to feel
good.
Happy.
Excited.

The look on Blaze's face
told me he felt
good.
Happy.
Excited.

But when we walked into
the lobby of the hotel
and I saw a happy family—
a mom, a dad,
and two girls—
I felt scared.
Sad.
Confused.

I watched
as the girls each took
their father's hands in theirs,
pulling on them,
as they begged him
to take them
to the Space Needle.

He laughed,
then gathered them
up and into his arms
and told them
he promised to take them
in the morning.

I thought of Blaze
holding me
and caressing me,
and told myself
it would make everything
better.

After all,
the world outside
the MarQueen Hotel
would surely
disappear
while we lost ourselves
in each other.

But as I looked around
the lovely lobby,
I knew we would end up
back there to check out
and head home.

And that's when
it hit me.

No matter what changed
in a hotel room
between me and Blaze,
everything else
would stay
exactly
the
same.

I need to believe

When I told him I wasn't ready,
and that I might have been doing it
for all the wrong reasons,
he told me he understood.
He told me I needed to be 100 percent sure.
He told me he would wait until I was 100 percent sure.

"You're really okay with it?" I asked him
as we sat in the car before going home.

He shrugged.
"I love you.
So I'm okay with it.
As long as it's *you* making the decision.
Not your dad.
Not your friends.
And most of all,
not the everyone's-a-sinner preacher at your church."

"Come on.
It's not even like that at my church.
How can you talk like that when you don't know?
You've never even been."

"I know I don't need God, Ali.
And I don't need a bunch of people telling me I need
God."

"You make it sound like God is a bad guy.
He's not bad."

Blaze sighed as he started the car. "Let's get you home."

As we drove in silence,
panic expanded
in my chest
until I almost
couldn't breathe.

First Claire.
Then Dad.
Now Blaze.

I reached over,
took his hand,
and placed it on my
rapidly beating heart.

"Please tell me we're okay," I whispered.

He pulled the car over
to the side of the road,
reached over, and kissed me—
a long,
slow,
wet,
beautiful
kiss.

"We're better than okay," he told me.
"Believe me?"

And of course,
I did.

Because the other choice
was pretty much
unthinkable.

trying to understand

Blaze's dad
was a bad, bad
beast
of a man.

Blaze hasn't told
me a lot.

But enough
for me to know
he was hurt
on a regular basis
and has
a few scars
to show for it,
though more inside
than out.

I think he
blames
God,
because it's hard
to blame
the one
who really
deserves it.

What I believe
is that life
is music and fabulous fall foliage,
but it's also cancer and wars.

That's just how it is.

Maybe God could do better.

But shit, so could we.

doesn't fit

The next morning
when I woke up,
I called Blaze
to tell him how much
I loved him
and appreciated him.

I told him
a lot of guys
wouldn't have been
as understanding
as he was.

He said
that's because
a lot of guys
are assholes
and he swore to himself
he'd never be
like that.

After we hung up,
I found Dad
on the couch,
holding Ivy.

Just him
and her.

I watched them
from around the corner.

He stroked her head.
He played with her feet.
He picked her up
and held her tightly
against him.

Part of me
wanted desperately
to join them,
while another part
wanted to turn and run
and never
come
back.

When I was little,
I loved doing puzzles.

There was this
ABC puzzle
I played with
all the time.

I always got the
M and the *N* mixed up.

I'd try
and try
and try
to get the
M to fit in the *N* spot.

I'd spin it
this way
and that way
until I finally
got up
and walked away.

Right then,
in that moment,
watching them together,
I felt like the *M*
trying to fit
in the *N* spot.

And once again,
I walked away.

broken

I was in the kitchen
getting cereal
when Victoria came in.

She held
a little frilly
yellow dress.

"Isn't this the cutest, Ali?
We're going to dress her up and go to the store."

I listened to them
giggle and squeal
as they got Ivy ready
for her first trip
to the grocery store.

You'd have thought
they were flying to
Ireland
to meet Bono.

After they left,
I felt so alone,
and all I wanted
was to talk
to my best friend
about everything
that had happened.

I got up the nerve to call,
but her cell phone
went right to voice mail.

When I called her house,
her mom said
she wasn't there.

The way she said it,
I knew
it wasn't
the truth.

The anger
and the sadness
and the hurt
came out
like a bullet
as I flung
my cell
across the room,
where it hit the wall
with a
loud
BANG.

Pieces
on
the
floor.

How
appropriate.

imagine

But what if her mom
wasn't lying?

Maybe Claire was
coming to see *me*.

Maybe I would
skip outside
to greet her.

Maybe we'd
go out
for coffee and doughnuts.

Best friends,
like before,
making music,
not war.

And then I remembered,
she'd rather make
bowling shirts
than make music
with me.

desolate

The driveway
stayed as empty
as my heart
felt.

a tangled web indeed

I had a sudden urge
to see pictures
of my family
together.

The happy family
I knew we were
years ago.

I searched
everywhere
for the photo albums.

In closets,
in cupboards,
in drawers.

The longer I looked,
the more frantic I got.

When I didn't think
there was anywhere else
to look,
I thought of
the attic.

I went up
and pulled on the string,
lighting up the rafters
and the cobwebs.

Way back in the corner,
partly covered with an old,
paint-spattered sheet,
was her stuff.

How sad that her
most-beloved possessions
were stuck in the corner
with the spiders,
like they were
creepy and unwanted.

Well, I love spiders,
thank you very much.

I threw the sheet back,
ran my hand across the desk,
and pulled on the top drawer handle.

Locked.

Drawer
after drawer
pulled open.

The photo albums
were in the bottom drawer.

After I took the albums out,
something shiny
caught my eye.
A tiny silver key for the top drawer,
carefully taped for safekeeping.

Carefully put there
for me.

ahoy, matey

I felt
like a pirate
discovering
secret
buried treasure.

Better than diamonds
or gold coins
or silver trinkets,
I found
sketches.

Mom's sketches.
My sketches.

Mine.

motherly love

In my room
I carefully
unrolled them.

My hand
oh-so-gently
caressed
each one as I
imagined
her hand there,
creating the images
she held
in her head
and her heart.

And in fact,
the first sketch
was a huge heart,
with a woman
holding a baby
drawn inside
of the heart.

The second sketch
was of a young girl
sitting in a chair
reading a book.

The third sketch
was the one
that brought tears to my eyes.

A sketch
of my face
and her face
side by side.

Together.

I wasn't sure
what they all meant
exactly,
but what I felt
and knew with my
whole being
was that she
loved being my mother.

And even if
she's gone,
that knowledge
can stay with me
forever.

a lover of news, I am not

I didn't notice
how quickly time
passed.

Suddenly
Victoria was there,
standing beside my bed,
looking at the sketches
I didn't want anyone
to see.

"Don't you knock?" I asked.

"Sorry.
Wow.
Are those—"

In one quick swoop,
I rolled them up
so they were
safe in my arms.
Safe from her.

"They're nothing.
Just a project I'm working on.
For school."

"Ah. Okay."

Dad came in.
"Everything okay?"

"Yeah," she said.
"I was just coming in to tell Ali the news."

I don't like
news.
I'm not a news
person.

News
is rarely good.

When do you
watch the news?

When something
horrible is happening,
like a tornado
or a blizzard
or a terrorist attack.

It's usually something bad
that makes you turn on
the news.

She told me, "We've decided we're going on a trip.
To visit my parents, in Chico.
Over Thanksgiving break."

"'We' as in 'you three,' right?"

Dad said, "No, Ali. All of us.
We're a family."

Yep.
I knew it.
Something bad.
Very, very bad.

one strange plot twist

I started an e-mail to Claire
ten different ways
and nothing seemed
right.

If I said,
"I'm sorry,"
it felt like I was saying
I needed to change
who I am
as a person *and*
as a songwriter,
and I didn't believe that.

If I said,
"Let's go to the church
and tell them
we want to keep playing,"
I was setting myself up
for a big fight
all over again.

It was like
I'd turned the page
in a book I'd loved
since the beginning,
and suddenly
it had turned into
a horror novel.

I wanted to slam the book closed
and run away.

Except
I'd grown to love
the main character's
best friend
so much,
of course I couldn't really
do that.

I had to keep reading
and find out what happened.

I just had to.

suffocating in silence

I skipped church
Sunday morning
because I didn't want to see her there
without fixing things first.

I stayed home,
writing a song,
wishing her to appear
with every
other
note.

The happy family below
carried on like it was only them,
just as it
should
be.

I skipped meals,
and they didn't
even
notice.

Sunday night
I looked out the window,
but the rain
drowned out
the stars.

My angel
was nowhere
in sight.

I curled up
with my oxygen tank
and tried
to
keep
on
b r e a t h i n g.

miles apart

The days passed
slowly
and
painfully.

With each day
the distance
between me
and Claire
grew
by miles.

It was like . . .

Monday in
San Diego

Tuesday in
Phoenix

Wednesday in
Baton Rouge

Thursday in
Atlanta

Friday in
Orlando

Man, it was lonely
at Disney World
all
by
myself.

I hate bowling

On Friday, while I was in Orlando,
sitting alone at lunch,
reading a book,
Claire sat with the popular kids.

But that's not the worst of it.

She sat with the popular kids,
wearing
a bowling shirt.

byob

Saturday morning
Dad took a drink
from a glass
in the fridge.

"This milk tastes funny," he said.

I turned and looked,
to see which glass
he was holding.

"That's breast milk, Dad."

"Why isn't it in a bottle?" he asked.

Because
obviously,
her breasts
are much larger
than her brain.

brain-radio

I missed Blaze
like a bee
trapped indoors
misses flowers.

He was swamped
at work because
two people
were out sick.

Saturday afternoon
I drove across town
to bring him
lunch.

A brown bag
filled with
a turkey sandwich,
an apple,
and chocolate chip cookies
made with a pinch of love
and a dash of tenderness
thrown in
especially by me.

Victoria
tried to convince me
to make oatmeal and raisin
because they're
my dad's favorite.

I wanted to say,
Make some yourself,
you slacker.

Instead I said,
"Chocolate beats raisins all the way."

When I got to the shop,
I saw him there,
behind the window,
behind the counter,
behind his beautiful smile,
talking with two girls.

I walked in and said,
"Blaze?"
with fire in my voice
from the flames
in my heart.

"Hey, beautiful," he said.

The girls stared
as I walked over,
leaned in,
and gave him a
nice, long
kiss
right in front of them.

"I brought you lunch.
You hungry?"

He nodded
and licked
his kissable
lips.

The girls
got the hint
and tiptoed past me,
as if any loud,
sudden
movement
would send me
reeling.

Another guy
came to take over the register,
then Blaze waved at me
to follow him.

As we walked,
I felt them around me.
Elvis, Fleetwood Mac,
Van Morrison,
AC/DC, the Eagles,
the Red Hot Chili Peppers.

If music is
the story
of our lives,
what song
did they
sing
for me?

The two songs
that popped into
my head first were
"Burning Love" and
"Love Will Keep Us Alive."

Then I remembered
that soon
we'd be leaving
for California.

"Highway to Hell"
started playing
loud and clear
inside
my
brain.

the cookie monster

He devoured the lunch,
then he devoured
my neck,
my ears,
my lips,
licking,
nibbling,
kissing
behind the closed
office
door.

"Those cookies were so good," he whispered.

And the way he looked at me
with love
and lust
and longing . . .
I told him with a smile,
"I don't think I'm making cookies for you anymore."

autumn perfection

Outside,
the air was cool
and crisp,
the way you want your sheets
when it's blistering
hot.

We walked to the park
and ran through the leaves,
picking them up
and throwing them at each other,
as if they were snowballs.

Instead of loud splats,
we got quiet flutters
of crimson and amber.

He pulled me to him,
spun me around,
and we fell
into a bed of foliage
fit for a king.

I wanted to freeze
the moment
in my mind
forever,
because there's nothing better
than flutters
of the heart.

lucky number seven

When he held me close,
out of breath,
leaves stuck to our jackets,
I whispered,
"I'm going to California in two days."

He whispered back,
"And in seven days, you'll be back home again.
With me.
And maybe being apart will make you want me like I
want you."

I laughed because he's
such a *guy*
and you can't blame him
for trying.

"Yes," I told him.
"In seven days I'll be home again."

"So count to seven instead of two," he said.
"Seven's better anyway."

And then he proceeded to give me
seven
amazing
kisses
just to
prove it.

they should be admitted

As I drove back home,
I thought about
driving in our old Isuzu Trooper
all that way
with the three of them.

Later, I asked Dad
if he thought it was
just a little crazy
to take an almost newborn
on a long car trip.

"Why? She'll sleep most of the way.
We'll stop every few hours so Vic can nurse her.
With stops, we figure it'll be a twelve-hour trip.
It'll be fine.
Her parents really want to see their granddaughter."

"Right.
So why do I have to go?"

"They want to see you too, Ali."

The whole thing
wasn't just a little crazy.

It was absolutely
insane.

absence makes the heart more desperate

Sunday morning
I got dressed
and went to church.

On the way there,
I prayed for a lot of things.

I prayed I could talk to Claire.

I prayed she'd listen.

I prayed she'd want to talk to me.

I prayed we'd be rushing to say "Sorry" first.

I prayed the distance between us
would disappear as soon as we hugged,
because we really are
best friends forever.

I prayed
and I prayed
and I prayed.

But when I got there,
Claire was nowhere
to be found.

making up is hard to do

And so
there was nothing to do
but go to her house
after church
and get her to talk to me
so we could end
this ridiculous fight,
or whatever it was
between us.

But on the way I realized
if she wanted to see me,
to talk to me,
she'd have been at church
like I was.

I mean,
that's been our thing—
to go there
together.

Wouldn't she
have made some kind
of effort,
if making up
was important
to her?

I drove
slower
and slower,
trying to decide
if I should go
or not.

Confused.

Then Dad called.
He asked me to stop at the store
and get snacks
and other necessities
for the road trip.

That's all it took
to help me make up my mind.

If she wanted to see me,
she knew where to find me.

At least until the next day,
when I'd be
on the road
to nowhere fast.

take the kitchen sink over me

I discovered
when you're going
on a trip
with a baby,
the whole
flippin' house
has to come along too.

But then I realized
if we just kept
packing it in,
maybe
there wouldn't be
any room left
for
me!

better pack the Goo Goo Dolls CD

There
was
room.

Right
next
to
the
car
seat.

good-bye, my Blazing Boy

Sunday night
Blaze came over
after work
to see me
before we left
bright and early
Monday morning.

As we walked
down the sidewalk,
bundled up,
arm in arm,
I told him
about Claire
and asked him
to check in with her
for me.

He told me
I was worrying too much
and I was probably
making more out of it
than I needed to.

He stopped walking,
turned,
and kissed me.

Goose bumps
rose
up
and
down
my body.

"I'm gonna miss you so much," he whispered
as he nuzzled my neck.

I looked up at the moon,
a silvery slice hanging there
like a shiny ornament
on a Christmas tree.

"Me too," I whispered back.
"I don't want to go."

"Who knows," he said,
curling my hair with his finger,
"maybe you'll have fun.
Vic seems pretty nice."

It was so funny,
I couldn't help but
tilt my head back
and laugh out loud.

"You are crazy," he said,
pulling me to him
and kissing me
again.

Crazy in love
was all.

pacifier is my new middle name

We left
before the sun
even peeked
its head out
from underneath
the covers.

I wished
I could have stayed
in my bed,
peaceful and warm.

After we dropped Cobain off
at the kennel,
we drank coffee
and ate doughnuts.

Then I tried to go
back to sleep.

It became obvious
fairly quickly
the baby
was
NOT
going to sleep
most of the way.

I put my earbuds in
and cranked the tunes.

A couple of times
Victoria asked me
to try to do something
to get Ivy
to stop crying.

Reluctantly,
I gave her my pinky
to suck on.

But when my arm
got tired
and I moved it away,
she started crying
again.

Victoria and Dad
looked at me
like I was supposed to keep
my pinky
in her mouth
forever.

I turned the music up,
rested my head against the window,
and pretended to sleep
like a baby should
and a bratty teenager
does.

two words: Holiday Inn

Imagine
a matchbox
with a broken match
dividing it up
into tiny rooms,
and you have
a pretty good picture
of their house.

After kisses and hugs
that smelled like garlic and wine,
Victoria's mom, Linda, said,
"Let me show you to your room."

Room. Singular.
One room
for two adults,
one baby,
and a
cussing-under-her-breath
teenager.

"You don't mind the floor, do you, Ali?" Victoria asked me.

Like I had a choice.

A sleeping bag
magically appeared
from the pile of stuff
we had brought.

They knew.

They could have made
reservations somewhere,
and they chose
not to.

That's when I was thinking,
who are these people
and what the hell
am I doing with them?

keep it coming

When the baby wasn't crying,
Dad was snoring.

I took my sleeping bag
and moved to the couch.

Around 5 a.m.
I discovered
Ted and Linda
are the type of people
who enjoy
greeting the sun
with a cup of coffee.

So much
for sleeping in
over break.

As I sat up
and considered
hitchhiking home,
Linda asked me
if I liked cream or sugar
with my coffee.

"Just cream," I said.

And then a vision
popped into my brain
of her finding a glass
in the fridge
and pouring it into
my cup.

I couldn't help it.
I jumped up to check.

She held a carton of cream
and poured some
into my big,
steaming mug.

It was probably
one of the best
cups of coffee
I'd ever had.

I decided if she'd just
keep the coffee coming,
maybe,
just maybe,
I could survive.

no fair

For two days
and two nights
we stayed in the
teeny-tiny house,
playing cards
and watching movies.

My guitar
was in the car
because I insisted
on bringing it,
but I was embarrassed to play it
in front of everyone.

So there was nothing else to do.

I had never
ever
ever
ever
ever
been
so
completely
bored.

Even Dad
was starting to look
like he was plagued
with cabin fever.

Which is probably why
he didn't argue at all
when his boss called him
and told him
he had to
fly to New York
on Thanksgiving night
and meet with a lawyer
first thing
Friday morning.

"Can I go with you?" I asked him.
"I've always wanted to see New York."

He shook his head
and told me
I had to stay with
Victoria and Ivy
because she might need help
on the drive home.

Wonderful.

"Did you know this might happen, Dad?" I asked.

"Yeah.
I mean, with my job, it's always a possibility."

It suddenly made
perfect sense
why they forced me
to come along.

happy thanksgiving

At Linda's suggestion,
we went around the table
and said what we were thankful for.

There was only one rule.
Once something was said,
it couldn't be said again.

Linda said family.
Ted said football.
Dad said health.
Victoria said Ivy.

Eyes turned to me.
Some eyes were curious,
some eyes were hopeful,
and it felt like
some eyes were disapproving.

Whatever they were,
they were all on me.
And when I said
the word "Blaze,"
four eyes looked confused
and four others looked embarrassed.

"My boyfriend," I mumbled,
to at least make the confused
less so.

They nodded
and smiled,
then Ted jumped up and said,
"Okay, let's cut the bird, shall we?"

So we gobbled the turkey,
got stuffed on the stuffing,
and ended on a sweet note
with fresh pumpkin pie.

After dinner
Linda brought out gifts
wrapped up in
paper splattered with
Santas, snowmen,
and angels.

I wondered if her calendar
was on the wrong month.

She told us
to take them home
and put them
under our tree
since we wouldn't be seeing them
for Christmas.

They'd be going to
North Carolina
to visit Victoria's brother
and sister-in-law.

Dad threw the box of gifts
in the back of the Trooper
before he left for the airport.

I got a quick good-bye,
while Victoria and the baby
got a lingering one outside
as Ted waited in the car
to drive Dad to the airport.

When Victoria came inside,
I noticed the tears on her face
before she retreated
to her room.

Linda said, "Come on, Ali.
Let's play rummy."

Man.
Dad was
so
lucky.

missing you

Thursday night
Victoria let me
borrow her cell phone
so I could call Blaze,
since I hadn't yet
replaced my old one.

He told me
how much he missed me
and that he'd just been working,
except not on Thanksgiving
since the store was closed
for the holiday.

He told me
how he slept until noon,
woke up,
watched football all afternoon,
then ate dinner
with his family.

Sounded
perfect
to me.

I asked him
about Claire,
and he said
they talked
and he'd tell me
more when I got home.

"Tell me now. Please?"

"Oh, Al, I don't know.
She's being weird.
I told her to stop it.
We kind of got in a fight, to be honest."

I felt my stomach
tighten at those words.

"When you get back, you'll work it out," he said.

"Tell me again how much you miss me," I said softly,
wanting that to carry me until I got back home.

He said,
"Like a tree misses its leaves
as it stands bare and naked
in the dead of winter."

Big. Sigh.

"We need to write a song together," I told him.
"You're so good with words."

"You're on," he said.
"But only if we make it hot and sexy."

I laughed.
"You're so persistent."

"One of my best qualities," he said.

"Then go use it on Claire.
And tell her to be my friend again."

let's go

It was decided
Friday night
over turkey sandwiches
and turkey noodle soup
we'd be heading home
Saturday morning.

Although not quite winter yet,
the forecasters were saying
Mother Nature
was planning
a spectacular preview.

So Victoria wanted to leave
before it hit.

Of course
there was no argument
from me.

When I woke up at 5 a.m.
for the fifth day in a row,
I was so tired,

all the coffee
in the world
couldn't help me.

I rummaged through
the medicine cabinet
while the water
in the shower heated up.

Tylenol PM
jumped out at me,
and I decided
it was my
perfect solution
for a peaceful
ride home.

I took two,
then let the water
in the shower
wash over me
as I thought
of Blaze
and Cobain
and Claire,
and how Dorothy was so right.

There's no place like home.

sleepyheads

Once settled in the car
and on the road,
Ivy fell fast asleep,
perhaps aware
of how badly
we both wanted her
to do just that.

And I
was right
behind her,
ready to dream
of being safe
in Blaze's arms
once
again.

awake

The first thing
I noticed
before I opened my eyes
was that my bladder
felt like it was going
to burst.

The second thing
I noticed
before I opened my eyes
was Victoria
cussing as she revved
the engine.

The third thing
I noticed
before I opened my eyes
was that we weren't
moving.

My eyes
flew
OPEN.

Out the window
it looked so strange,
I blinked,
and blinked again.

It didn't look
real.

Like at home
when I turn out the light
in my room
and all I see
is blackness.

It was snow,
falling so hard,
all I could see
was whiteness.

Whiteout.

this can't be happening

As if sensing
the sheer panic
I was feeling,
Ivy started crying.

Without thinking,
I stuck my pinky
in her mouth.

"Victoria, please tell me I'm dreaming."

And then
Victoria started crying.

It didn't go on long
before I yelled,
"Stop it!
God, you're not helping."

She turned around,
bit her lip,
sniffled, and nodded.

Then she reached back
and unlatched Ivy
from her car seat,
pulling her close,
like a little girl
looking to her doll
for comfort.

Victoria started talking
faster than
my heart was beating.

Something about
a bad wreck on the freeway
near the Oregon border,
so she turned off
to take the back roads
that she drove with Dad last summer.

She babbled on
about the snow
coming harder and harder,
stopping to feed Ivy,
then continuing on,
going down winding back roads for miles,
trying to find her way.

"And now," she said, finally slowing her words down,
"we seem to be—"

"Stuck," I said, since she hesitated to say the word.
"So call someone."

She pointed her pink phone at me.
"It's dead.
You used it last night, and I forgot my charger."

I shook my head,
trying to get this new piece
of information
to sink in,
but I had to pee so bad,
I couldn't even think.

"What time is it?" I asked.

"Three."

Damn.
Guess I was tired.

"Why didn't you wake me?" I asked her.

"Like you could have helped," she said,
in a tone that totally irritated me.

I grabbed my coat
from the back
and put it on.

"Where are you going?" she asked.

"To the bathroom," I mumbled.

When I jumped out of the car,
the cold slapped my face
as the snow
devoured my boot-covered feet,
and it was as if
I'd come face to face
with a
freaking
frosted
monster.

A monster,
I hoped,
who would get tired of us
and would very quickly
let us
go.

day one

I tried to push the car out
with Victoria at the wheel.

No luck.

She tried to push the car out
with me at the wheel.

No luck.

Again
and again
we tried.

No luck.
No luck.
No luck.

Dad always said
people in Seattle
who had fancy SUVs
with four-wheel drive
were paranoid,
since it only snows,
like, once a year there.

Well, I wished he had been
a bit more paranoid
about us going on a
million-mile road trip
with a baby.

Without four-wheel drive,
getting out
seemed
impossible.

Ivy wailed,
her cries
a reflection
of what we
were feeling.

We collapsed
in the car,
trying to melt
the icicles on our hands
that used to be fingers.

It wasn't until
warm tears
stung my frozen face
that I realized
Ivy wasn't the only one
crying.

heated

Sadness
quickly became
red,
hot
anger,
despite
the bitter cold
around us.

I tried to hold it in,
but it was like trying to
keep a lit firecracker
inside a cardboard box.

"How the hell did this happen?" I yelled.
"I don't get it!
One minute,
we're driving down
the damn freeway.
And the next,
we're in the middle of nowhere,
stuck in a blizzard?
Are you really that freaking stupid?"

Sizzling.
Scorching.
Hot.

"Okay, stop it!" she screamed.
"The storm came out of nowhere.
And all the roads started to look the same.
It's not my fault, Alice.
It's not!"

"What the—
Then who the hell's fault is it?
Mine?
Is it my freaking fault?"

Silence.

I laughed.
"You're going to blame this on me, aren't you?
I bet you're plotting right now
what you're going to say to Dad
to turn him against me even more.
Well, how about this?
Why don't you
just throw me
out there to freeze to death?
Then you could have
your nice little family
without me.

Or I know,
I'll make it easy for you!
I'll just go."

Burning.
Boiling.
Hot.

I started to reach back
for my guitar,
because where I go, it goes,
but Victoria grabbed my arm
and pulled me back to my seat.
Hard.

"You listen to me, Ali," she hissed.
"I'm not plotting anything.
And you're not going anywhere.
You're staying here,
and we're going to figure this out.
Together.
And I want you to know something.
Just because you hate me doesn't mean I hate you.
I've tried my best—"

"What?
Your best?
Come on, you haven't tried your best
to do anything.
Most of the time, you ignore me.
How is that trying?"

Searing.
Steaming.
Hot.

"I don't ignore you!
I leave you alone
because you make it clear that's what you want.
You miss your mom.
I get that.
But don't make me out to be some terrible person.
Because I'm not."

She took a deep breath,
her eyes closing as her
tongue curled up
like I'd seen it do so many times before.
She blinked, and blinked again.
But it didn't help.
The tears started to come.

"Of course it's my fault
we're in this Goddamn mess," she cried.
"Is that what you need to hear?
You want to hear how bad I feel,
knowing I've done this to you?
To Ivy?
To all of us?"

She wiped her face
with the back of her hand,
then pointed at me.

"Right now, it's you and me.
We have to work together,
whether you like it or not.
And regardless of how you feel about me,
I'll do everything I can to get you home."

Through the whole
heated exchange,
Ivy had stayed glued
to her chest,
clutched hard,
like a pillow
after a terrible
nightmare.

When it got quiet,
I watched
as Victoria
gently
and lovingly
loosened her grip,
raised the baby up,
and tenderly kissed
her teeny-tiny
face.

I leaned over,
closed my eyes,
and put my warm cheek
against
the glass.

Freezing.
Frosty.
Cold.

into the night

Black
replaced
white.

Silence
replaced
shouting.

Fear
replaced
anger.

We kept the car on
for a while,
then turned it off
to save the gas we had
so we could get out
when we were able.

Victoria and I
took turns
holding Ivy,
making quiet
exchanges,
the tension
in the car
thicker
than the snowdrifts
outside.

She spoke first,
in barely a whisper.

"I'm sorry, Alice.
We'll be okay.
I promise you.
We will."

I started to argue,
but before I did,
I thought of Claire
and how an apology
from one of us
would have kept the crack
from turning into a
canyon.

It wasn't the time
to grow further apart.

I pulled out
a bag of chips
and tore it open.

"Dinner?" I asked.

the good and the bad

There was
one small container of formula
and two baby bottles
Victoria brought along
in case we needed to feed Ivy
and couldn't stop somewhere.

Good.

There were three
bottles of water
and one can of Diet Dr Pepper
I bought at the store
before we left.

Pretty good.

There was one sleeping bag
for two and a half people.

Pretty bad.

There were two small bags of chips
and one candy bar
for two hungry people.

Bad.

We each had a couple of chips
and a bite of candy bar
for dinner,
followed by
some sips of water.

"Somebody will find us," she told me
as I slid into the sleeping bag
to take the first shift of sleep.

My stomach
grumbled a reply of
"I sure as hell hope so."

this isn't Hollywood

I don't think
there has ever been
a night
longer than
that first night
in all
of
eternity.

We took turns
curling up
on the backseat
in the sleeping bag,
although it might as well have been called
the tossing-and-turning bag
because I don't think
either one of us
actually slept.

Ivy slept
in fits and starts
underneath the layers of clothes
and three blankets
she was swaddled in.

We turned the car on
throughout the night
and ran the heat.

As I lay there,
dreaming of home,
I thought of the movie
The Snowman,
where the snowman
takes the little boy
and flies through the air.

Too bad
real life
is never anything
like the movies.

from scared to petrified

When the darkness faded
and a grayish light
filled the sky,
we saw
that the monster
had grown
to gigantic proportions
overnight.

Not only
had it not
let us go,
but it had
completely
and totally
devoured us.

We were
savagely trapped
in the snowy belly
of the beast.

day two

We managed
to make it out
to the tree
that had become
Mother Nature's bathroom,
but the snow
was now up to our knees.

When the snow started to dump
on us again,
my hungry stomach
tightened up in response,
knowing
the snow
would only get
deeper
and deeper.

"We have to do something," I cried
after a breakfast of Diet Dr Pepper
and a lunch of a few chips.
"We can't just sit here and wait.
Can't we build a fire or something?
So planes will see us?"

"Do you have a match?" she asked me.

"No, but—"

"But what?
We just have to wait.
They'll go looking for us
when we don't show up today.
They will.
And they'll find us."

"Isn't the cigarette lighter
from the car in here somewhere?
Check the glove box."

While she looked,
I jumped in the back of the car,
tossing items,
searching,
desperate to find something
we could use.

And that's when I saw
the brightly wrapped
Christmas presents.

merry Christmas early

She didn't find
the lighter.

I opened Ivy's big gift,
with lots of colorful paper,
which would be
the most helpful.

I ripped carefully,
trying to keep it
as whole as possible,
to wave in the air
like a big flag.

It was an antique stool,
a few nicks
here and there,
obviously
lovingly used.

Victoria reached over
and ran her hand over it,
like it was a beloved pet.

"The stool my grandma gave me," she said.
"They kept it all this time."

An image
of a little girl
named Ivy
toddling up to the stool
to wash her hands
flashed through my brain.

Before that moment,
I hadn't pictured her
as anything
but a little,
annoying blob.

But in an instant,
I saw what I couldn't see,
and it was
wonderful
and sad
all at the same time.

Next I opened
the gift for Dad.
A bottle of his favorite
brandy.

Victoria opened the bottle
and took a swig.
She handed it to me.
I took a whiff
and the smell
sent shivers
through my body.

I put the cap on
and decided I'd save it
for a more desperate
moment.

When I got to my present,
I paused before I opened it,
hoping it would be something
really useful
in the coming hours.

I gasped
when I saw the antique book,
the cover worn and
corners frayed,
a musty smell to it.

Carefully
I opened
the front cover.

1897.

Incredible.

My own antique edition
of *Alice's Adventures in Wonderland.*

Truly amazing,
although not very helpful
unless we could slip into
the rabbit hole
and find our way home.

I realized
Victoria must have told
her mother that
my parents named me
after Alice.

I was snapped out of my
wonderland trance
when Victoria asked,
"May I open mine?"

I handed her the tiny box,
which wouldn't do us much good
as far as wrapping paper
was concerned.

Inside
lay a gold locket
with a tiny picture
of Ivy inside.

She slipped it on,
then gave the locket
a little
kiss.

"For luck," she whispered.

If only it were
that easy.

hocus-pocus

Like three-year-olds being silly,
we put socks on our hands
and underwear on our heads,
because we hadn't thought
we'd need
gloves and hats
in California.

Then we stepped outside
and waved
our red and green paper
through the white frosty air,
with the hope
that someone would fly by
and see us.

The trees stood above us,
their branches a canopy
that kept us
from seeing
much of the sky
at all.

As I waved the paper
through the whiteness,
I thought of Mom
swirling her brush of paint
across the white canvas,
turning nothing
into something
magical.

And I wished
for some of that
colorful magic
to come
to us.

failed miserably

It wasn't long
before our
crisp, vibrant paper flags
became a soggy mess,
like tulips in a flower bed
pummeled
by an unexpected
hailstorm.

We threw the paper
on the ground
in defeat.

I took the white underwear
off my head
as we trudged back
to the car.

I twirled it around
on my finger,
as if waving
a different
kind of flag.

The kind that says

we
    surrender.

a first

While we sat there,
trying to warm up again,
Vic asked me
how my phone
broke.

And so
I told her
the whole
ugly story
of me
and Claire.

She listened,
asking the right questions
in the right places,
like a good lawyer
in a courtroom.

And yet
I didn't feel her
judging me.

Instead
what I felt
was her
trying
to understand me.

getting to know you

Over the course
of a couple of hours,
I learned
Vic's favorite meal
is meatloaf with mashed potatoes.
But she never makes it
because Dad told her
I hate meatloaf.

I learned
her favorite movie
is *Sleepless in Seattle* with Tom Hanks,
which I've never seen.
She told me we'd watch it together
when we got home.

I learned
she was starting to miss
her accounting job
and hoped to go back to work
part time when Ivy
turned four months old.

I learned
some other stuff,
but mostly
I learned
she's pretty easy
to talk to.

Kumbaya

Vic reached over
and grabbed my guitar.

"Did your dad get you this?"

I shook my head.
"It was my mom's."

She handed it to me.
"Why don't you play something?"

I strummed
a couple of chords,
then tweaked a jingle
Dad and I had made up
about a cheap wine he likes.

"When your car is stuck
and you're out of luck
and there's no tow truck
in sight,
and you're horror struck
and a sitting duck,
drink Three Buck Chuck
all night!"

She laughed.
"I could go for a bottle of that about now."

It was quiet for a minute.

"I wonder what Dad's doing," I said softly.

She reached over
and touched my arm.
"Everything he can to find us."

I nodded.
She was right.
She had to be.

"Okay, now, let's sing some campfire songs," she said.

And so,
with no fire,
except the one
we kept dreaming about,
I played
and we sang.

answers

After two days
of little food
and lots of stress,
Victoria's milk
started to wane.

Ivy didn't like
the cold formula
very well.

It made
Vic
more worried
than she had been.

When darkness came,
I held the baby
as Victoria tried
to sleep,
and I noticed
Ivy's
teeny
tiny
fingers.

Tiny
little
icicles
I tried to warm
in my
hands.

I remembered the
day Claire asked me
all the questions
about her.

I thought,
If I could answer her now,
I would tell her:

Yes, she's cute.

She looks like my dad,
with his flat nose
and dimple in his chin.

She has lots of dark hair.

And Claire,
although you didn't ask me,
I've come to learn
that I love
holding her
in my arms,
even if I pray as I do,
Please keep her safe
Please keep her safe
Please keep her safe . . .

dreaming

I drifted
in and out of sleep,
dreaming of
doughnuts with coconut
and warm, smooth coffee.

I dreamt of music
in church,
of a voice
that filled me with
joy,
love,
and hope.

I dreamt of
warm kisses
from a hot boy
with a burning flame
for me in his heart.

When I woke up,
the warmth vanished
faster than a bubble
that's been

popped.

melting hearts

The clock on the dashboard
said 5:07 when it was time
for another dose of heat.

I thought back
to waking up
on the couch
at five in the morning
in the matchbox house,
and what I wouldn't give
to be back there
again.

Vic and I
exchanged some words
about how much
we did and didn't sleep
and joked about
breakfast.

I ordered pancakes with bacon,
while she thought a
a Spanish omelet
sounded good.

Then
it was deathly quiet
in the darkness
until she said,
"Ali, I want you to know, um—
I really do love your father. A lot."

"I know."

"And I'm sorry if I've hurt you.
It's all new to me.
Like it is to you."

She sounded
sincere.

"From what he tells me," she went on,
"your mom was a great woman."

She paused.
Then she said,
"She sounds like someone I would have liked."

Ivy started to fuss,
so Vic pulled up her sweater
and put her there,
secretly hoping,
I'm sure,
that Ivy was getting
more than just comfort.

"She was awesome," I whispered
as we listened to Ivy's
little suckling sounds.

"You know those sketches?" I continued.
"On my bed that day?
Those were hers.
I found them, locked in her desk."

"Really?
Why were they were locked away?"

I'd thought about that.
About what that meant,
and why she didn't give them to me,
even if they weren't finished.

I think it's like my music.

"Sometimes it's just too personal," I told Vic.

I think she drew
those sketches at a time
when she was really hurting.

Thinking about leaving me
and wishing,
on paper,
she didn't have to.

Kinda like
my songs.

Me writing them,
thinking about her leaving me,
and wishing,
through music,
she didn't have to.

Except maybe
Claire was right.

Maybe I've been wishing
long enough.

I hope he knows

As snow filled the air,
Blaze filled my thoughts.

With every breath,
my heart ached
to see him again,
to touch him again,
to hold him again.

What if
I never saw him again?

Did he know
how much I loved him?

Did he
really
and truly
know?

Victoria noticed
when quiet tears
trickled out.

"Ali?"

"I should have done it."

"Done what?"

"He got us a hotel room.
On his birthday.
But I couldn't do it."

She put Ivy
in her car seat,
then moved over
so she sat
next to me.

"I just hope he knows
how much I love him," I told her.

"Ali," she said,
"you don't do it to prove your love.
Saying no means you love yourself *and* him.
Besides, he obviously adores you.
He let you decide.
And it didn't change anything between you.
Right?"

I nodded.

"The way you look at him?" she said,
wrapping her arm around me
and pulling me to her.
"He knows.
Believe me, he knows."

day three

The snow
was getting
deeper
and
deeper.

The air
was getting
colder
and
colder.

Our spirits
were getting
lower
and
l
    o
       w
         e
           r.

"I have to go for help," Victoria said,
looking out the window
at the vast display of whiteness.

"You won't make it.
It's too cold."

She looked at me.
"I have to try.
If I don't, none of us will make it."

I offered to go,
so it was me
making the sacrifice
instead of her.

But she shook her head.
"No. I got us into this.
I'll get us out."

"Victoria, you're Ivy's mother.
She needs you.
She needs your milk.
I *have* to go.
Don't argue.
I'm going."

I started to pull out clothes to wear,
when she grabbed my arm.

I had never seen her
so stern.

"Ali, I don't have much milk left.
And besides, it doesn't matter.
I'm the grown-up here.
I can't send you out there.
I can't.
It has to be me."

I looked at her,
at Ivy,
and then
at the monster
outside.

It felt like
my insides
were being ripped
out of my chest.

"Don't go," I sobbed.
"Just stay here.
They'll find us, like you said.
They will.
We have to stay together."

She shook her head again.
"If they haven't found us by now,
it means we're hard to find.
I'm going.
And you will stay and take care of Ivy.
You can do it."

Good thing
Confident
was her middle name,
because it certainly
wasn't
mine.

out of our cold hands

We put layer
upon layer
of clothes
on her,
along with my
boots.

I hoped
those boots
would be as good to her
as they had been
to me.

She had brought her heavy coat,
which we were thankful for.

I searched the car
to see if there was anything
else she could take
to help her
on her journey.

Wishful thinking.

Why didn't Dad
put a roadside
emergency kit
in the car?

How could we travel
all that way
and not have one?

I kept searching,
and when my hand
touched something
hard and cold,
underneath the backseat,
I pulled it out.

A flashlight.

It wasn't a lot.
But it was something.

"Are you sure you don't want it?" Vic asked me.
"You might be scared by yourself."

I shook my head
and placed it in her hand,
mine wrapping around hers
for just a second.

I made her eat
the rest of the chips
before she left,
and she drank lots of water
plus a little brandy.

We talked about Ivy
and keeping her fed
and warm
and all the other things
a baby needs.

When she looked at me,
her tongue curled up,
I saw fear
in her eyes.

But I saw
determination there
too.

And when she looked at her baby daughter,
I didn't see a tongue-curling chameleon anymore.

I saw
one thing
and one thing
only.

A kind,
loving
mother.

I thought of my mom
and how hard she fought
with love
in her heart
for us.

Maybe it's not about
determination
or love
or how hard
you can fight.

Maybe it's just about
fate
and what is meant
to be.

And so,
when I really
didn't know what to say,
I told her,
"Good luck,"
as she hugged me good-bye.

Because
that was probably what
she needed most
in that moment.

"If I don't make it—"

"Don't talk like that," I told her.
"You'll find help and you'll get us out of here."

Then it occurred to me
she probably needed
something else
in that moment.

"Dad would be proud of you, Vic.
He loves you. He really does."

She nodded.

"Come back to us," I said.

I really,
really
meant it.

gone

I watched her walk
until her silhouette
was swallowed up
by the forest
and there was
once again
nothing to see
but white.

Words and a melody
popped into my brain—
a song
asking to be
written.

I grabbed my guitar
and sang it out loud to Ivy,
who watched and listened,
like she totally loved it.

"Walking away with love in your heart,
hoping the coldness won't keep us apart.

"Playing the memories like songs in my head.
Things we've shared and words we've said.

"Don't drift away.
I want you to stay.
Don't drift away.
You really should stay.
Don't drift away.
Please . . .
come back to stay."

a snow-angel friend

The formula,
the water,
and the food
weren't the only things
we'd been stingy with.

We'd been treating the diapers
like a precious commodity,
making Ivy wear them
as long as possible.

When we went to our
make-believe
outhouse in the snow,
we took the used diapers
with us.

Ivy drifted off to sleep,
so I used the opportunity
to bundle up
and head to our
special tree,
diaper in hand.

The clouds above
had cleared slightly
and the snow
had stopped falling
for the moment.

I took just a second
to appreciate
the pure beauty
around me.

I felt sad
that I couldn't
enjoy it
by building a snowman
or making snow angels.

And then I thought,
Why can't I?

I flopped down on the ground
into the fresh powder,
my arms and legs
gliding back and forth.

When I stood up,
I looked down at the angel,
white and delicate,
like lace.

A guardian angel
for us.

alice in winter wonderland

In the afternoon,
when Ivy started fussing
and I'd fed her
some formula
and there was nothing else
I could do,
I pulled out the antique book
and started reading.

My voice
or the story
or something
calmed her,
and so we settled in.

I read about Alice
d
r
o
p
p
i
n
g
down the rabbit hole
and growing small
and growing big
and growing small again.

Alice was
by herself
down that hole.

She wanted
to follow
the rabbit
so bad,
but she wasn't able to.

I'm pretty sure
I knew
exactly
how she felt.

from bad to worse

So thirsty,
I drank
the last few drops
of remaining water.

My hand
became a shovel
as I scooped snow
into one of Ivy's
bottles.

It seemed somewhat
ironic that what could kill us
would now keep us
alive.

Except,
I quickly discovered,
there would be no heat
if the car
wouldn't start.

And without heat,
there would be
no water.

grow wings, little one

Every hour
it got colder.

I felt it
when I went out
to the bathroom.

I tried
on and off
into the evening
to start the car.

Even though
it still had
some gas,
it just wouldn't
start.

Too
freaking
cold.

Ivy
fell into
a deep sleep.

I put her
in the sleeping bag
and thought of her
as a caterpillar,
snuggled up
in her cocoon.

I watched her,
then closed my eyes
and saw
a little girl,
her brown hair
flapping in the wind,
the yellow sun
kissing her face
as she ran around
in our yard.

Sleep,
little one,
sleep.

Grow strong,
and grow wings.

The world
is waiting for you.

sometimes prayers do work

Like an old man
waking from a long nap,
the motor sputtered and coughed,
and finally turned over.

Like an old woman
coming inside from a rainstorm,
I breathed a sigh of relief.

After I melted the snow,
I took a couple sips
of water
and then I made Ivy
a bottle.

I had never been
so glad
to see a bottle
completely
emptied.

believe

Help did not come
like I hoped it would.

Darkness
surrounded us,
and without Victoria
there to talk to,
the silence
was almost
maddening.

I thought of her
walking alone
in the dark
and I wanted to scream
from all the fear,
anger,
and sadness I felt.

I would start to imagine
the worst,
but then I'd make myself imagine
a different picture.

It looked something like this:

She will use
the flashlight
to find a sheltered spot
where she can sleep
for the night.

She will
think of us,
and that will keep her strong.

She will
miss feeling her baby in her arms,
and that will push her on.

She will
find help tomorrow,
and that will get us home.

still breathing

In the middle
of the night
the bitter cold
took hold of us,
squeezing us so tightly,
I shivered in pain.

The car
was dead
again.

As I cuddled with Ivy
in the sleeping bag,
trying to keep her warm,
I thought of Cobain,
my oxygen tank.

God, I missed him.
I missed his warm, silky fur,
his smelly dog kisses,
but most of all,
the way he calmed me.

I tried to pretend
he was there with us.

I breathed.
She breathed.
I breathed.
She breathed.

My hand
stroked her little head
full of dark hair.

She let out a big sigh,
and although I couldn't see her
in the blackness of the night,
I knew she was calm.

And with that
realization
came another one.

It wasn't
about me
anymore.

a light

Drifting in and out of sleep,
I heard a soft voice
whisper my name.

I sat up,
startled to hear something
aside from Ivy's
baby noises.

A soft,
glowing light
appeared
outside.

I squinted my eyes,
straining to see
who or what
it was.

Was it Victoria,
coming back?

I couldn't tell,
but the light
floated closer to me,
literally floating
through the nighttime air.

An intense feeling
of comfort
and warmth
washed over me,
as if God himself
had joined us.

I longed
to be closer.

But as I reached down
to open the door,
the light disappeared,
leaving us in the
cold,
lonely
darkness
once again.

all alone

No.
Victoria!

Don't leave me.

Oh God,
no.

Am I all
Ivy
has left?

what was it?

An angel.
Coming to check on us.
Coming to check on
her baby.

It's all
that makes
sense.

I stayed awake
last night,
with only my memories
to keep me company,
waiting for her
to return.

She never did.

part 2

with angels
we will fly

day four, continued

Like the North Star,
ever present in the sky,
regret shines brightly
in my soul.

That regret,
combined with the recent events,
make me cry and cry
until there are
no tears left.

As I look back
over the past weeks,
I wish I could change
so many things.

But I can't.
The past is gone.

Uncertainty
about tomorrow
hangs in the air,
now even more noticeable
than the cold.

I hold Ivy close,
thinking of her mother,
wanting to believe
last night
didn't happen,
and that she's still out there,
alive and well.

But I *know* it happened,
as sure as I know
there is only one thing
we can do
now.

I whisper into Ivy's ear,
"Take it one minute at a time.
That's all we can do.
Hang on one minute at a time."

really empty

I fasted at church one time
for twenty-four hours
to raise money
for the local food pantry.

They wanted us to know
what it feels like
to have that pain deep inside you
and no way to make it stop.

Of course,
that was ridiculous
because we did make it stop
at the end of the twenty-four hours
when we had a huge
pizza fest.

But now I *really* know
what it feels like.

And it sucks.
A lot.

I think of Vic,
who was out there,
stomach gurgling
as she walked alone
in the frigid air.

And I know
I've got
nothing
to complain about.

are you there, God?

Luckily
I'm able to get the car
started again.

I decide
I can't turn
it off
anymore.

It must stay on
until every last drop
of
gas
is
gone.

Please let someone find us today.
Before it's too late.

a glove-box breakfast

Desperate to find
something else to eat,
I empty the
glove compartment,
hoping some food
will magically appear.

A pile of napkins
proves my theory
that Dad has a
serious addiction
to Jamba Juice.

I find two packets of ketchup
and an old, green Life Savers candy.

It's not coffee and doughnuts,
but I'll take it.

After I suck the ketchup
out of the packets,
I reach for my
tasty dessert,
only to
d
r
o
p
the candy
between the seat
and the center console.

I push my hand
deeper and deeper,
oblivious to the pain.

I want to laugh at
the irony
of feeling like
my life is dependent
on a candy called
Life Savers.

coming undone

I can't reach it,
no matter how hard I try,
and the tears come
because I want that candy
so damn bad.

The wave
of emotion
grows
bigger and bigger,
becoming a
tsunami
as I pound the seat
with my fist
over
       and over
and over
       and over
and over,
       harder
and harder
       and harder
and harder
       and harder,

until my hand hurts
and I SCREEEEEEEAAAAM
from the pain
of the moment
and all of the
horrific,
painful moments
leading up to this one.

When my screams
become more of a whimper,
I hear Ivy bawling,
and look back
to see her
bright red face,
and her whole body
shaking.

And suddenly
it's all too much,
and I wonder
if we shouldn't just
GO.

Maybe we would find help.
Maybe we would make it.
Maybe it's the only chance we have.

I scoop her up
and sit in the front seat,
rocking her back and forth,
back and forth,
back and forth,
talking as I rock.

"Should we go, baby?
Should we?
Would we be okay?
Would we?
I don't know what to do.
What do I do?
Stay here and die?
Go out there and die?
What?
WHAT SHOULD I DO?"

The weight of everything
is so much,
I can't even hold us up
anymore.

I crumble to the
cramped space
in front of the seat,
both of us
crying
shaking
broken-hearted
fed up
ready
to be rid
of it all
for good.

it's a deal

In a ball
curled up
holding tight
feeling sad
praying hard
feeling mad
making plans
feeling bad
reaching deep
underneath the seat
trying
one
last
time.

If I get it,
we stay.

If I don't,
we go.

deals were meant to be broken

My hand
touches something.

Something *bigger*
than a Life Savers candy.

Something *better*
than a Life Savers candy.

A *true*
lifesaver.

The car's cigarette lighter.

ignited

I use my
sock-covered hands
to carve out
a place
in the snow.

When the orange light
touches the paper napkin,
it creates a flicker of a flame,
which creeps up the side,
somewhat hesitantly,
but still, it moves,
until finally
the flame
grows larger.

Slowly I add more napkins,
pine needles,
and wrapping paper.

It smolders,
burns,
and finally,
ignites.

Fire.

I quickly collect sticks
and sprinkle them
with brandy.

The fire crackles
and grows,
bigger still.

More sticks.
More brandy.

I search the car
for burnable items.

My eyes
land on the book,
and I think,
there must be
something bigger.

The stool is there,
full of memories
and dreams,
ready to create more
in the coming
years.

I reach for it,
hesitation swirling
through my fingertips.

How can I turn
those dreams
into ashes?

And yet,
do I have
any other choice?

A child
without a stool
is much better
than
a stool
without
a child.

in the eyes of the beholder

Orange and red flames
dance cheek-to-cheek,
making me want to dance,
and so I do.

I twirl,
twist,
jump,
yelling while I do,
"Take that, you freaking frosted monster!"

For the first time,
I am controlling
the monster
more than it's
controlling me.

I search for something
that will create
lots of smoke.

Smoke that
will reach the sky

and let people know
we are here.

I spy
the small pile
of used diapers
by the tree trunk.

Underneath the
big fir branches,
they've stayed fairly dry.

One by one,
they're thrown into
the snapping
flames.

Dark,
gray
smoke
floats
to the sky.

Ugly to many.

So very
beautiful
to me.

what's in a name

I watch the fire burn
from inside the car,
my warm breath
creating a foggy spot
on the window.

I write my name
with my fingertip,
like I did
when I was little.

A L I C E

It's then I notice
the word
"ice"
in my name.

How
appropriate.

lost

As the fire burns,
Alice
and the Caterpillar
and the White Rabbit
keep us company.

My mother
told me her favorite part
of the book one time,
but I can't remember
what it was.

I flip
the pages,
looking,
searching
for a piece of my mother
in the story.

It feels
hopeless.

As I watch
the sun
slip away
for the night,
and the flames
of the fire fade,
hopelessness
is
a
feeling
more
and
more
familiar
to
me.

I reach
for my guitar.

My constant companion
through the sad and lonely times.

As I think of Victoria,
my dad, and Blaze,
the hopelessness is so strong,
I can taste it.

My fingers strum,
and I hum a tune.
There are no words
for what I'm feeling
inside.

Smoke
and music
fill the air.

There is
no choice.

In the morning
they'll be one,
rising together
to create
a beautiful
melody
called
Hope.

by the numbers

VICTORIA:

one bottle of water

four layers of clothes

ten frozen fingers and toes

forty-eight hours of icy hell

US:

one fire burning

two warm bodies in the sleeping bag

six bottles of formula

forty pages of *Alice in Wonderland*

Numbers don't lie.
She should have stayed with us.
We made a mistake.

A mistake
we will all pay for

one million times over.

I am . . .

Tired
of the
cold

Tired
of the
hunger

Tired
of the
deadly
silence

I am
so
very
tired

I
want
to
rest

day five

When I wake up,
early in the morning,
the sun barely
visible
and the blackness
disappearing
just enough
so I can see,
I go outside
and look
for the angel I made.

She's gone,
of course,
covered by
fresh, new snow.

I make another one.

When I'm done,
I don't get up.

I stay there
and dream of
flying away
to the place
where angels
live happily
ever
after.

far from you

My wings lift me
out of the snow,
above the trees,
into the clouds.

My wings carry me
to a place where
all is washed clean
and there is light.

My wings give me
a view of you,
afraid of the shadows,
alone in the cold.

My wings show me
when I'm far from you;
it's like an icicle
through my heart.

My wings return me
to the soft patch of snow
where the sun shines brightly
and love brighter still.

a message

And then
the real angel visits again,
her light
illuminating the world
around me.

I try to see her face,
but she appears to be
faceless.

Warmth engulfs
and soothes me,
like a warm bubble bath
on a cold winter's night.

She whispers my name.

"Alice."

I can't make my lips
say her name.

"Don't give up," she says so softly,
I can hardly hear her.
"Help is coming."

Then, as quickly
as she appeared,
she's gone again.

one last try

After seeing
the angel again,
a surge of energy
fuels me.

Ivy's cries
pull me up
to face reality
one more time.

I make another fire,
and throw part of my
heart on it
when I break my guitar
against a tree
and place it there.

Heartbroken.

The orange flames
pop and grow,
blazing brightly.

I feel Blaze's presence
in the fire,
and it gives me strength.

I think back
to when Vic and I
sang campfire songs.

I wish she were here
to sing with me now.

As the fire burns,
wood turning to ash,
death fills my mind,
and I swear to myself
there can be
no more.

When the fire
is big and strong,
I place the floor mats there,
to make more
dark smoke.

It works.

I kneel by the fire,
thinking of Victoria
and all she
must have endured,
and hate myself
for not making her stay.

When the car
runs out of gas
a little while later,
I feed Ivy
the last
of the formula.
And then I strip us down
so I can give her
the heat of my body
in the sleeping bag.

As I hold her
and look
at her little eyes,
her little nose,
her little mouth,
and her little fingers and toes,
I remember my mother's words.

Find the gift in the little things.
And remember, I am with you always.

I didn't see the gift.

Just like I didn't see
the angel made of stars
in the painting at first,
I didn't see the gift in Ivy.

But I do now.

And I want to enjoy the gift
for years
and years
to come.

at last

Ivy and I
are sleeping,
deep inside
the sleeping bag,
when I hear
something.

Is it the angel?
Has she come back?

Like that morning
weeks ago,
I don't open my eyes.
I don't move.
I don't speak.

Every part of me
seems to be
frozen.

"Ali, sweetheart, we're here.
Hang on, honey.
Just hang on."

Dad?

Am I dreaming?

up, up, and away

There is lots of noise.
There is the feeling of flying.
There is my body being poked and prodded,
and warmth and tingling.

There is me thinking, I did it.
I made it.

There is also me wondering,
Am I the
only
one?

floating

A warm pillow
holds my head.

A warm hand
holds mine.

A warm voice
speaks to me.

I float
in the warmth.

Like I'm
floating along
on a warm,
soft cloud.

I like
it here.

Safe.
Soft.
Warm.

holding on

She visits me.
She rubs my back.
She kisses my cheek.

My angel.

She is as clear as the sky
on a winter day
when the storm has passed
and all that's left
is baby blue.

"Did they make it?" I ask.

"Alice, you have to go back."

"Please tell me. I have to know."

She pulls me to her,
holds me,
and strokes my hair,
just like I did
with Ivy.

"You were so brave," she whispers.

Tears spring
from nowhere
and everywhere.

My heart cries the loudest.

I don't want to face the truth.
I don't want to go back.

I don't want to leave
my angel
of a mother.

torn

"I miss you," I cry.
"I miss you so much."

She holds me
like she used to
before bedtime.

The words
from her painting
sing in my brain.

I am with you always

But it makes me mad
because it's
not really
true.

I squeeze her,
wanting to hold on forever,
afraid of what will happen
when I let go.

Finally
she pulls away,
but I clutch
her hand tightly
in mine.

"I don't want to go," I tell her.

She cups my chin
with her other hand,
and her soft eyes
hug mine.

"You don't belong here, honey."

"But Mom, I'm losing you.
It's getting harder and harder to find you."

She kisses my forehead.
"Honey, no matter where you are, I'm with you.
When the breeze brushes your cheek, that's me.
When the stars sparkle and shine, that's me.
When the tulips bloom in the spring, that's me."

The little things.

She's there,
in the little things.

Voices
from far away
shake me.

Dad calls
my name.

She squeezes my hand and says,
"It's time to go.
But I'll be with you."

"Mom, what was your favorite part in *Alice in
Wonderland*?
I can't remember, and I have to know."

"It's a famous line of Alice's.
About going back to yesterday.
You'll find it. When you get home."

Home.
Where I belong.
With Dad.
With Blaze.
With Claire.
With Ivy (I hope).
Home.

And then
I'm floating again.

Falling
and floating
through a sky
filled with love.

So much love.
Everywhere.

I land softly
next to Dad,
where he whispers in my ear,
"Don't leave me, Ali.
Please.
I can't lose you, too."

part 3

family keeps us warm

gone but not forgotten

The light lingers,
but then
begins
to
fade.

Lighter
and lighter,
softer
and softer,
until
it disappears
completely.

baby, oh baby

My eyes
flutter open
and meet his.

Tears
of joy
pour
forth.
"Ali," he whispers.

"Is she—?" I croak.

"What, honey?
What do you need?"

"Ivy," I say.

A kiss
on my forehead,
his stubble
tickling
my skin.

"She's fine," he tells me,
tears still falling
from his face to my pillow.
"You kept her safe.
And I'm so proud of you."

My eyes close
as I try to keep
my own tears
contained.

But there is one more question
that lingers.

I start to say it.
I start to say
the other name
I'm thinking of.

But I can't
because I know
his tears of joy
will quickly turn
to tears of grief.

And I have already
seen enough of those
to last
ten lifetimes.

wishing

Dad puts a straw
into my mouth
and I sip.

The cool water
soothes my throat.

But not the pain I feel.

I wish I hadn't had a fight with Claire.
I wish I hadn't broken my phone.
I wish I hadn't fallen asleep while we drove.
I wish I'd found the lighter sooner.
I wish I'd made her stay.
I wish
I wish
I wish . . .

She probably
took a thousand
painful steps
for a baby
who will never know
her mother.

A thousand
painful steps
for me.

I wish I'd
taken those steps
instead.

what did you say?

I close my eyes,
tighter this time,
like that morning
so long ago
when they left
for the hospital.

Who was that person
so angry at Dad
for loving again?

Dad reaches over,
says to me,
"And Ali,
Victoria—"

"No," I gasp,
my voice hoarse.

Another
forehead kiss,
and a smoothing
of my hair
by his strong hand.

"Sweetheart," he whispers,
"she's okay."

My eyes
pop open,
needing to see
his lips
speak the
words I thought
I heard.

"What?
What did you say?"

"She's alive.
She found help.
And she helped us find you."

This time
I don't try
to contain
my tears.

I
just
let
them
f
a
l
l

like

s   o   f   a   e
    n   w   l   k   s

order, please

The IV
pumps fluids
through my veins.

The longer I am awake,
the hungrier I get.

The nurse asks me
to choose from the menu.

I ask her,
"Can I have it all?"

Dad laughs at that,
and then he says,
"I guess she's going to be just fine."

melting

When Blaze walks in,
any coldness
that remains
melts completely
away.

Nothing
has ever looked
so good,
so perfect,
so absolutely
hot.

The nurse
is checking my vitals,
so he waits
for her to finish.

I want to ask her
if my heart rate
shot up
at the sight
of my boyfriend,
but I don't.

I don't have to ask anyway.
I know it did.
He does that to me.
He's always done that to me.

After she leaves,
he is there,
on my bed,
holding me and
kissing
every inch
of my face.

"God, Ali.
I thought I'd lost you."

"Shhhhhh," I tell him.
"Don't talk.
Not yet.
Just hold me.
Please.
Just hold me."

And so
he does.

Because
that
is what I missed
most of all.

answered prayers

After lots of holding,
I tell him
about our days
in the car,
about chips and ketchup,
which kept us nourished,
and the sleeping bag
that kept us warm,
and the guitar I burned
that kept us hopeful,
and the story of Alice
that kept us company,
and how it's all of that
and so much more
that kept us
alive.

He shivers
at times,
like he's in the car
with us.

I shiver
at times,
because it's hard
reliving it all again.

When I'm finished,
he tells me
how search teams were formed,
how he begged to go and help,
but his mom
wouldn't let him go,
so he walked around in a daze,
unable to eat or sleep or work.

We're quiet for a minute,
mentally walking
in the other one's
shoes.

He kisses me.

A long,
warm,
soft
kiss
that reminds me
of watching
a pink-and-orange sunset
as the fireflies appear.

When we're done,
he pulls out the key chain.

"Ali, every day,
I held this,
and I prayed you'd come back to me."

"Really?"

He shrugs.
"Who else could I turn to?"

I smile, and ask him,
"So does that mean you'll go to church with me
sometime?"

He laughs and says,
"You know what? Maybe I will."

confused

I'm not ready
for Blaze to leave,
but he says
he needs to run an errand
for his mom.

I tell him
to hurry back.

He's only gone
for a minute.

I laugh.
"I knew you couldn't stay away long."

He smiles.
"Claire's here.
She brought you doughnuts."

I think of her
standing there,
doughnuts in hand.

I want to be happy,
but instead
I feel my heart
droop like a daisy
at night.

She didn't
want to make up
before.

She didn't want
to talk it out.

She didn't want
to be my friend.

I broke my phone
because of her.

A phone that could have
saved us
from all
that we endured.

I don't get
why she's here.

She thought I was dead,
so now she loves me again?

"I'm not ready to see her," I tell him.

Because it's the truth.
I'm not.

time to start stitching

A little while later,
Dad walks in
carrying Ivy.

I squeal
when I see her.

He places her
in my arms,
and I can't believe
how good
and strong
and healthy
she looks.

"Ali," he says, "I need to tell you how sorry I am."

My eyes move
from the baby
to him.
I can tell
it's hard for him.

"I pushed you away," he continues.
"You remind me so much of your mom.
And it hurt, I guess."

"I didn't exactly make it easy for you."
It's not all your fault."

Ivy is kicking her legs,
waving her arms,
and looking at me with her
big, beautiful eyes.

Thankfulness
oozes from my pores.

She is here.
She is strong.
She is fine.

"It's so weird how much I love her now," I say.
"I guess something good did come out of being lost.
I'm just sorry it took a stupid crisis."

"I don't think it matters *how* hearts are mended, Al.
Just that they are, you know?"

I think of Claire,
going home,
an expert mender
when it comes to clothes,
but unable to mend
her broken heart
without my help.

She has the needle,
but I have the thread.

"Can I borrow your phone, Dad?"

the best medicine

Blaze and Claire
walk in
at the same time.

Claire is still holding
the bag of doughnuts.

And Blaze is holding
a brand-new,
supersweet
guitar.

"Blaze! Seriously?"

He puts it in my lap
and gives me a kiss.

"Figured you'd want to start writing.
And playing.
I know that's how you deal with stuff."

I look at Claire.
"I'm sorry, Ali," she says.
"You can write whatever songs you want."

I smile at her.
"No.
You were right.
People don't want to feel sad all the time.
I've learned I sure as hell don't."

She comes over,
gives me a hug,
kisses my cheek,
and hands me my
doughnuts.

"I've missed you so much," she says
with tears in her eyes.

"Me too," I tell her.
"And I'm sorry too.
For everything."

She hugs me again,
and when she stands up,
she says, "So come on.
Pass out the doughnuts!
I'm starving."

I strum on my guitar,
then hand it to Blaze
so I can eat.

Doughnuts.
Music.
Love.

It doesn't get
any better
than this.

clear skies

Ivy and I
are both released.

Vic has to stay
a little longer
because she lost some toes
and needs to start
rehabilitation.

When I visit her
before we go,
she's holding
her sleeping baby,
and the picture
of the two of them
is just how it should be.

She pats the edge
of her bed
and asks me
to sit with her.

"I don't know how you did it," I tell her.

"Me neither," she says.
"I just walked and walked,
even when I didn't think I could go any further.
It's a miracle the search team found me.
I think an angel was looking out for me."

When she says that,
I can only nod
because I know
it's true for all of us.

Outside the window
there is blue sky,
sunshine,
and fluffy white clouds.

In a few minutes
I'll be out there
again.

Will I ever
think of the world
the same
again?

Will I ever
squeal in delight
at the sight of snow
again?

Her voice jars me
from my thoughts.

"Thank you, Ali.
For taking care of her."

I reach over
and grab Ivy's
little hand.

I don't want to worry.
I don't want to be sad.
I have so much to be happy about.

So I smile and say,
"Next time I baby-sit,
can we have a pizza delivered?"

helicopter dog

Cobain
is there
as I open the door,
and I think
he might lift himself
off the ground,
his tail
is wagging
so hard.

discoveries

It's dinnertime,
and Dad asks me
if I want to
help him make enchiladas.

I see the can of sauce
on the kitchen counter,
and I remember the jingle
we made up
together.

As soon as I
start singing,
he joins in.

"Sweet Fiesta Verde Sauce,
Verde Sauce,
Verde Sauce.
Sweet Fiesta Verde Sauce,
Frankenstein's lip gloss!"

We laugh when we get
to the final line,
and I tell him
enchiladas sound great.

But then Ivy cries
and I instinctively
reach down
and pick her up
to comfort her.

After a few seconds,
her mouth curves into
a big grin.

"Dad, she smiled!
She smiled at me!"

I talk
baby talk to her
and she keeps smiling.

"That grin's bigger than the Cheshire-Cat's," Dad says.

And then I remember.

"Did the car make it back here?
Or the stuff in the car?"

He shakes his head.
"Not yet.
Why?"

My brain is thinking,
trying to remember
if I have another copy.

"Can you make dinner by yourself?
Ivy and I want to look for something."

"Of course," he says.

When I find the book
on my bookcase,
I flip through the pages,
wondering how
I will ever know
which part is
Mom's favorite.

Something about
yesterday.

Flipping
skimming
flipping
skimming.

And then
a mark in the book
catches my eye.

It's underlined.
Did she do that?
Has it been there this whole time,
and I never noticed?

I read the line out loud.
"'. . . it's no use going back to yesterday,
because I was a different person then.'"

"I guess it means
everything's always changing," I tell Ivy.
"Nothing's ever the same."

I stop and grab
a piece of paper,
lyrics coming at me
faster than my hand
can write them down.

Inspired.

As I write,
it's as if Mom is there
next to me.

She understands.
She always did.

And suddenly
I feel the need
to go to my closet,
get the painting she gave me,
and place it on my desk.

"You know what?" I say to Ivy
as I think about our time in the snow.
"The more you can share,
the less lost you feel."

flying through the rabbit hole

a song
by Alice Andreeson

Everything's always changing.
Nothing stays the same.
Yesterday's gone forever,
I've got memories and my name.

But like Alice I grow bigger,
and I shrink back, yes, it's true.
It's the ebbs and flows of life,
it's the rabbit hole we go through.

But with angels we will make it.
And with angels we will fly.
We will keep on going forward.
We will fly, yes, we will fly.
We will fly, yes, we will fly.

Friends will keep us happy.
Our family keeps us warm.
We'll party through the good times
and hold tight through the storms.

Because with angels we will make it.
And with angels we will fly.
We will keep on going forward.
We will fly, yes, we will fly.
We will fly, yes, we will fly.

Wonderland is here now.
Don't know what we might see.
Yesterday's gone forever.
But my future's up to me.

What a future it will be. . . .

Here's a look at Lisa's first verse novel:

I Heart You, You Haunt Me

Wishful Thinking

I'm sitting
on the porch swing,
thinking of how
Jackson and I
used to
sit and swing
together.

The stars are duller
than an old pocketknife.
They used to sparkle
like five-carat diamonds.

I wonder,
is heaven
up in the stars?
Beyond the stars?

Can Jackson see them
like I see them?

Is he wishing
like I'm wishing?

"Star light, star bright," he said the first time
we sat here together.

"Make my wish come true tonight," I said.

"That's not how it goes."

"Why drag it out?" I asked.

He laughed. "So, what's your wish?"

"That time would stop,
so we could stay like this forever."

"Tough wish," he said.

"What about you?" I asked.

"Let's see.
I'm hungry.
How about a cheeseburger?"

"How romantic," I told him.

"Change your wish to a chocolate shake and we're set."

We went to In-N-Out Burger after that.

He got his wish.

I didn't get mine.

I Need Mr. Sandman

Sleep doesn't come.
Night after night
I thrash around
like a fish
caught in a net
trying to escape.

And I cry
for what I've done
and who I've lost.

Four days after the funeral,
Mom shows me the phone messages
she's taken for me.

I didn't want to talk
to anyone.

Jackson's brother, Daniel, called.
Jessa and Zoe called.
Nick called,
again.

I ball them up
and throw them away.

"You're tired," Mom says.

She calls the doctor.
He prescribes Ambien.

"That's good," Mom says.
"Sleep will help."

Will anything *really* help?

When I wake up,
I remember.

It hurts
to remember.

Mom brings me a sandwich
and some juice.
I get up to pee
and sneak another pill.

"I need to sleep a little more," I tell Mom.

She doesn't argue.

Because sleep helps.

Company's Coming

The phone rings.
It rings and rings.
I finally drag
my butt out of bed
and answer it.

"Ava?"

"Yeah."

"Do you want to do something?" Cali asks.
"Maybe go to the pool?"

"Not really."

"Wanna do something else?"

"Not really."

"Are you okay?"

"Not really."

"Can I come over?"

"I guess."

"You need anything?"

But before I can answer, she says, "Never mind.
Stupid question."

Stupid.
But sweet.

Mirror, Mirror

I'm putting on makeup.
I'll be like a clown
and no one will see
the real face
behind the mask.

I don't want Cali to see
the sad me,
the depressed me,
the shamed me.

As I stand in the bathroom,
carefully lining my eyelids
bronze,
I feel a splash
of cool air.

I shiver.

I feel something.
Something behind me.
Something familiar.
Hauntingly familiar.

I glance behind me,
but I don't see
anything.
Or anyone.

And then,
when I look in the mirror
again,
I see,
for a split second,
not just me,
but someone else.

Jackson.

And don't miss the companion novel to
I Heart You, You Haunt Me:

Chasing Brooklyn

Gabe was one of those guys

who was full of life.
Always talking.
Always laughing.
Always wanting to be the center of attention.

Big guy
with a bigger smile
and the biggest heart.

After Lucca died,
it changed Gabe.
Of course it would.

He went from front and center
to just fading into the background.

We hung out for a while
after it happened.
Didn't talk much.
Mostly we sat in his room,
me writing letters,
him strumming on his guitar.

Still, we promised
we'd help each other through it.

But then, something changed.
I don't know what.
Was it him? Was it me?

He joined a different band.
Stopped coming around.
I just lost track.
We lost track.

I try to remember
the last time I saw Gabe
and I can't.

He didn't just fade
into the background.

He pretty much
disappeared.

#278

Dear Lucca,

Can you believe this? I can't.

I can't believe he's gone.

Remember that one time the three of us went to see Kings of Leon? Gabe sang every song. He knew every single song.

I seriously feel sick. Gonna go lie down.

Love always,
Brooklyn

Gabe and my brother

had been friends

since fourth grade.

They'd grown apart in high school

when Gabe chose music

and Lucca chose art.

Still, they had that connection,

the kind that stays strong

despite the differences.

No matter how long it'd been

since they'd seen each other,

they'd pick up right where they left off.

Gabe made Lucca laugh like no other.

Gabe with his wild hair that stuck every which way,

his pierced lip

and the black leather jacket

he wore everywhere.

He was a character.

A character who should still be here.

Damn it all to hell.

He should still be here.

I fall asleep hoping to dream

of Lucca.

Instead I'm standing in the hallway at school.
In the dark.
Alone.

I turn around
and around,
wondering where everyone is.

I want to turn on the lights,
but where do you find the lights
for a school hallway?

There's the faint sound of footsteps.
Someone is far away.
But coming closer.

I listen.
They get louder.

I open my mouth.
I try to speak.
Nothing comes out.

I walk forward,
my arms in front of me,
trying to see my way.

There's a faint light ahead.
I think it's the light to the office.
If I can just make it there,
it'll be okay.

The steps are coming faster.
My pace increases.
Just get to the office.
Nothing can hurt you there.
They'll help you.

The light gets brighter.
I start to run.
Faster and faster
I run,
the beating of my heart
almost as loud
as the pounding of my steps.

I reach the door and look behind me.
I see someone.
Someone's coming.
Right behind me.

I turn the doorknob.
Locked tight.

My fist pounds on the window.
I pound and pound
and open my mouth to scream.

Then, he's there.
In front of me.

Gray skin with eyes
black as the darkest night,
and lips blood red.

He lunges for me
and I scream his name.

"Gabe!"

When I wake up
with my sheets soaked
and sticking to me like bandages,
I can't stop shaking.

Even though I know it was a dream,
something about it
was so much more
than a dream.

A lot more.

Something happened last night

and I am freaking out.

It was almost morning. I was asleep.

I heard a noise.

A scraping noise.

I sat straight up and noticed the window was open, just slightly.

The room was freezing.

I ran to the window and closed it.

I was about to turn on the light, when I felt something.

Like someone was right there.

I lunged for the baseball bat under my bed and started swinging.

I made my way to the light and turned it on.

No one was there.

Nothing was there.

And yet, it was like someone or something *was* there.

And then I heard a whisper.

Not even a whisper.

Something else.

A silent message in my brain.

Make sure Brooklyn is okay.

The curtains fluttered.

A slight shadow emerged on the wall.

And then, he was gone.

The room warmed up.

My goose bumps disappeared.

And I ran out of my room.

Acknowledgments

Lindsey Leavitt and Lisa Madigan, you complete me. Thank you for your wisdom and insight, and your willingness to read at the drop of an e-mail. Sara Crowe, agent extraordinaire, a million times, thank you for all that you do. Michael del Rosario and the fine folks at Simon Pulse, I appreciate your efforts and hard work more than I can say. Scott, Sam, and Grant, thanks for your unwavering enthusiasm. I'm pretty sure when God was handing out families, He saved the best one for me. Kate, Deena, Emily, and Tina, my Author2Author blog buddies, thanks for letting me join you. I've learned so much from you! Sally, you are, and always will be, my jukebox hero, and I just want to say thanks for being my loving, supportive friend. Dan, Dolores, and Margie, thanks for the laughs and making work fun. To my friends in the LJ hood, thanks for being there through it all. Jason Wade, you don't know me and you'll probably never read this, but I just had to tell you that I'm not sure I could have written this book without your music in my ears.

Finally, thank YOU, wonderful reader. Thank you from the bottom, top, and sides of my ever-grateful heart.

ABOUT THE AUTHOR

LISA SCHROEDER is the author of *Far from You* and *I Heart You, You Haunt Me*, a 2009 ALA Quick Pick for Reluctant Young Adult Readers. She loves to write in verse because it allows her to really get at the emotional core of the story. She is grateful to all of the people who have read her books and told their friends about them, since being an author is more fun than ponies or water slides (most of the time, anyway). Lisa lives in Oregon with her husband and two sons. You can visit her online at LisaSchroederBooks.com.

calling all book clubs!

Get the chance to speak with an author after you and your friends have read her book.

If you're a member of a book club (classrooms count too!), enter to win **up to 25 books** for your group and a follow-up call from one of the participating authors:

Kate Brian   Deb Caletti

Angela Johnson

Lisa McMann   Lisa Schroeder

Elizabeth Scott

TO ENTER THE SWEEPSTAKES, VISIT:
simonandschuster.com/sweepstakes/call-me-book-club-sweepstakes
Winners will be selected in a random drawing from all eligible entries received on or about May 3, 2010.